NEW WRITING FROM THE CARIBBEAN

SELECTIONS FROM
The Caribbean Writer

Edited by
ERIKA J. WATERS

MACMILLAN
CARIBBEAN

For Francis and Blair

Selection and editorial matter © Erika J. Waters 1994
The stories are © their authors 1994

All rights reserved. No reproduction, copy or transmission of this publication may be made without written permission.

No paragraph of this publication may be reproduced, copied or transmitted save with written permission or in accordance with the provisions of the Copyright, Designs and Patents Act 1988, or under the terms of any licence permitting limited copying issued by the Copyright Licensing Agency, 90 Tottenham Court Road, London W1P 9HE.

Any person who does any unauthorised act in relation to this publication may be liable to criminal prosecution and civil claims for damages.

All characters in the stories are fictional, and any resemblance to actual persons, living or dead, is purely coincidental.

First published 1994

Published by THE MACMILLAN PRESS LTD
London and Basingstoke
Associated companies and representatives in Accra, Auckland, Delhi, Dublin, Gaborone, Hamburg, Harare, Hong Kong, Kuala Lumpur, Lagos, Manzini, Melbourne, Mexico City, Nairobi, New York, Singapore, Tokyo.

ISBN 0-333-58240-3

Printed in Hong Kong

A catalogue record for this book is available from the British Library.

Contents

Acknowledgements	iv
Introduction: Literary Magazines	v
PART I 'You Like Me Like You Like Rum and Cricket?': **Men and Women**	1
Lily, They Said, *Olive Senior*	3
Ah Liberated Man, *Marvin E. Williams*	11
Miss Joyce and Bobcat, *E. A. Markham*	27
PART II 'Dissa Pickney Mean fi Kill Me': Mothers, **Fathers and Children**	37
Baby, *Vjange Hazle*	39
The Occasional Sadhu, *Rabindranath Maharaj*	44
Pan for Pockot, *Lionel Seepaul*	53
The Dark Side of Being Nine, *Jonathan Small*	62
PART III 'This is What She Had Been Missing Without **Really Knowing': Home and Exile**	73
Exile, *Anthony Lockhart*	75
Flying the Flag, *John Gilmore*	82
Graduation, *Edwidge Danticat*	89
Antojos, *Julia Alvarez*	95
PART IV Questions and Essay Suggestions	109
A Note to Teachers	110
PART V Notes on the Authors	117

Acknowledgements

Sincere gratitude is due to Dr Darshan S. Padda, Vice-President for Research and Land Grant Affairs at the University of the Virgin Islands, for without his support and encouragement, *The Caribbean Writer* would not have existed. Thanks as well to President Orville Kean and Vice-President for Academic Affairs Dr Denis Paul for their support.

A special thank-you to Carlyna Allard, Carrol B. Fleming and Paul N. Brierley, along with other family and friends, who supported this project in various ways.

Acknowledgements are made to *The Caribbean Writer*, University of the Virgin Islands, which first published the stories reprinted here, except 'The Dark Side of Being Nine' and 'Flying the Flag'.

Olive Senior's story, 'Lily, They Said', from 'Lily, Lily', in *The Arrival of the Snake-Woman*, published by Longman Group UK, first appeared in an earlier version under the same name in *The Caribbean Writer* (1988). It is reprinted here courtesy of Longman Group, UK, copyright Olive Senior.

'Antojos' is from *How the Garcia Girls Lost Their Accents* by Julia Alvarez. Copyright Julia Alvarez, 1991. Published by Plume, an imprint of New American Library, a division of Penguin Books, USA, Inc. Hardcover edition originally published by Algonquin Books of Chapel Hill. First publication, in a somewhat different form, in *The Caribbean Writer*, 1990. Reprinted by permission of Susan Bergholz Literary Services, New York.

Introduction: Literary Magazines

Here are 11 new stories, undeniably different, stereotype-shattering stories, which deal with the problems we confront today. Mostly culled from the pages of *The Caribbean Writer*, they are provocative and engaging, bold strokes on a canvas drawn in the long, excellent tradition of Caribbean literary magazines.

For despite their size, literary magazines (small or 'little' magazines, as they are sometimes called), have played an inordinately large role in the Caribbean. The early magazines of the 1930s and 1940s were particularly receptive to new writers and launched many careers. In fact, 'with the exception of V. S. Naipaul and a few others,' Reinhard W. Sander has written, 'almost every significant West Indian novelist published his early work in these periodicals' (p. 438).

Sadly, however, until that point, the Caribbean had not provided a particularly nurturing environment for literature by Caribbean peoples. The high illiteracy rate, the traditionally oral folk culture, and the lack of publishing opportunities contributed to this situation. Alvona Alleyne, of the University of the West Indies, Jamaica, has ventured a more insidious reason. She notes the damage caused by 'the hostility of an educated class, who, because of their colonial-style education, with its stress on things European, believed that West Indians had no literary talent' (p. 222).

In a conscious effort to find a non-colonial voice, numerous little magazines were born during the social upheavals of the 1930s and 1940s. One editorial in Trinidad's *Beacon* clearly trumpeted the intention to dissociate themselves from the British, and A. J. Seymour wrote of the period at the end of the war when he started *Kyk-Over-Al*: 'Self-definition and self-discovery were in the air' (quoted in Morris, p. 4). These and other revolutionary magazines, the most famous of which was *Bim*, published stories and poems about Caribbean people and Caribbean landscape using Caribbean language, and they were edited by forward-thinking writers or teachers who persevered for both a love of literature and a sense of nationalism. These editors and their magazines provided emotional, intellectual and, on occasion, financial support for fledgling writers.

vi   New Writing from the Caribbean

According to Reinhard Sander, major magazines from this early period were *Trinidad* (1929–30), edited by Alfred H. Mendes and C. L. R. James; *The Beacon* (1931–33, 1939), edited by Albert Gomes; *Kyk-Over-Al* (1945–61), edited by A. J. Seymour, revived in the 1980s with Ian McDonald who now edits it alone; *Focus* (1943, 1948, 1956 and 1960), edited by Edna Manley; *Voices* (1964–66, 1969–70), edited by Clifford Sealey and *Bim* (1942–73), edited by Frank Collymore and since 1974 by John Wickham (Sander, p. 4).

Bim, from Barbados, is, by general consensus, preeminent among the magazines from this period. Poet and critic Mervyn Morris has called it 'the most important outlet for the Caribbean writer in English' (pp. 5–6), for many of the major writers publishing today, among them George Lamming, 1992 Nobel Laureate Derek Walcott, and Kamau Brathwaite were early contributors. Brathwaite, recalling his beginnings as a poet, has admitted that without *Bim*, he would have 'dried up'. '[*Bim* was there]', he has said, 'when I was a struggling writer and people were not supporting what I was doing and I couldn't get support from friends, family, critics or writers' (p. 74).

It is commonly accepted that *Bim*'s success was due to the generous personality and unceasing dedication of its editor, Frank Collymore, who once emphasised in a letter to Edward Baugh, of the University of the West Indies, that *Bim* was 'strictly non-political, non-racial, non-religious. . . . Our one policy has been through the years to encourage creative talent' (quoted in Morris, p. 6). Poet and critic John Figueroa calls Collymore simply 'a saint' (p. 73).

But how has the literary environment changed since the days of *Bim* – when, as Braithwaite has said – if Frank Collymore published your work in *Bim*, you were invited into his living-room, welcomed into his home?

The establishment and growth of Caribbean universities in the past thirty years has affected the literary landscape by supporting conferences and visiting writers and by publishing numerous journals and literary magazines. And although still not abundant, regional publishing houses are developing.

While *Bim* continues to be published, new literary magazines have also been founded. These include *Jamaica Journal, Tapia* (*Trinidad & Tobago Review*), *New Voices*, edited in Trinidad by Anson Gonsalvez; *Artrage*, edited in London; *Sargasso*, edited in Puerto Rico by Lowell Fiet; *Savacou*, edited in Jamaica by Kamau Brathwaite, which has appeared as the publication of the Caribbean Artists Movement since the 1960s; and *The Caribbean Writer*, which first published most of the stories in this collection.

The Caribbean Writer, sponsored by the University of the Virgin Islands, premiered in 1987, and while its mission was to feature new writers, from the beginning, the magazine had the support of many established writers who contributed their work, among them Olive Senior, John Figueroa and Derek Walcott. The large numbers of submissions from the region and abroad attest to the continuing need for new publishing opportunities.

In spite of the literary magazines and the universities, however, the pull of the metropolis remains strong, sometimes overpowering for writers, and the Caribbean diaspora is more wide-ranging today. The major English-language publishers with substantial distribution and promotion systems are still based in England and America, as are universities with vast resources, and a reading public that in sheer numbers surpasses anything possible in the Caribbean. The temptations are great, and the writers in this collection are a case in point. Here is a Trinidadian writer living in Canada, a Montserratian in England, a Haitian in Brooklyn.

But Caribbean writers, regardless of where they live, by their continued publication in Caribbean-based magazines, express their commitment and ongoing desire for a link with a readership that understands, often through nuance and humour, their language and their sensibility. Novice writers look to regional literary magazines as a realistic first step to wider publication, and the magazines function as muses, too, as many writers have admitted. The fact that there will be another issue the following year sustains many new writers who don't find success at first.

Not surprisingly, literary magazines enjoy a well-deserved reverence in the Caribbean. Few would deny that these magazines publish the most vibrant work available anywhere, placing vitality and originality above monetary reward and reputation, art above ambition.

*

New Writing from the Caribbean is divided into thematic units which reflect the major preoccupations of most human beings: the often-paradoxical relationships between men and women; the indescribable bond between parents and children; and the particular predicament of exile, so integral to Caribbean life. These themes often reflect the clash of generations or the battle between the sexes as Caribbean life has undergone such dramatic changes in recent years.

Part I portrays relationships from one extreme to the other, from the traditional to the modern. 'Miss Joyce and Bobcat', by E. A. Markham, reveals that sexual tensions continue throughout life and transcend social class. Olive Senior in 'Lily, They Said', which is part of her longer story published in *The Arrival of the Snake-Woman*, renders the old seduction story fresh and new through her unique language and style. 'Ah Liberated Man', by Marvin E. Williams, the story that won the Canute Brodhurst Prize in *The Caribbean Writer* for 1991, forges a new path for West Indian male–female relationships as the older ways become not only less viable but also less desirable for all concerned.

In contrast to nostalgic memories of childhood, the stories in Part II portray an unidealised view of Caribbean childhood. 'The Dark Side of Being Nine', by Jonathan Small, tells of a child's suicide and, another, 'Pan for Pockot', by Lionel Seepaul, of a young boy left to fend for himself in a macabre, almost surreal world. Vjange Hazle's 'Baby' portrays the jealousy of a childless midwife, shattering the selfless-soul stereotype and leaving us with a fully developed character. 'The Occasional Sadhu', by Rabindranath Maharaj, reveals child–parent relationships and the disastrous end of one family.

Part III shows both young and old West Indians abroad. In Edwidge Danticat's 'Graduation', the horrific memories of a young Haitian refugee return to haunt her, and in 'Flying the Flag', by John Gilmore, we are privy to the conflicted emotions of a young English boy toward his adopted West Indian home. Anthony Lockhart's 'Exile' reveals the London existence of a politician-turned-professor, and we witness the critical decision that shapes his future. In Julia Alvarez's 'Antojos', a story which was chosen for inclusion in *Editor's Choice III: Fiction, Poetry and Art from the U.S. Small Press*, an expatriate West Indian returns home to find her identity challenged and her loyalties confused.

What will strike the reader is that there are no clichéd plots, predictable endings or old, familiar characters in these stories, for they were chosen for their uniqueness and originality. Both topical and timeless, these are stories that speak of the Caribbean in a language like no other.

Works Cited

Alleyne, Alvona, 'Literary Publishing in the English-Speaking Caribbean', in *Twenty Years of Latin American Librarianship*. Final Report and Working Papers of the 21st Salalm, University of Indiana, Bloomington, 2–6 May 1976. Austin, Texas: Salalm Secretariat, 1978: pp. 222–48.

Brathwaite, Kamau, Interview with Erika J. Smilowitz, *The Caribbean Writer*, Vol. 5, (1991): pp. 73–8.

Figueroa, John, Interview with Erika J. Waters, *The Caribbean Writer*, Vol. 6 (1992): pp. 69–76.

Morris, Mervyn, 'Little Magazines in the Caribbean' (paper delivered at Literary Symposium, Carifesta, 1981, Barbados), *Bim*, 1984: pp. 3–9.

Sander, Reinhard W., 'Short Fiction in West Indian Periodicals: A Checklist', *World Literature Written in English*, November 1976, Vol. 15: pp. 438–62.

PART I

'You Like Me Like You Like Rum and Cricket?'

Men and Women

Lily, They Said

OLIVE SENIOR

Lily, they said, had the sweetest voice in the land, a pure soprano that could hit all the high notes and break crystal and startle birds. Lily sang not only in her own church, but was invited to concerts and socials and rallies at the churches around to sing sometimes with Mr Abbott, a baritone. Their voices blended perfectly with Aunt Mercy as chaperone. And because Lily was young and slender and beautiful all the young men would stand outside the post office even when it wasn't open, hoping to get a glimpse of her or hear her voice or the cascading notes of the piano. Sometimes in the wooden house by the river, Lily sang only for herself, totally unconscious of the commotion her singing caused. For instance: all the duppies in the graveyard who were getting ready to haunt people one night stopped dead in their tracks at Lily's singing. (It was the only thing that had any effect on them outside of garlic and asafoetida.) And Mr Shepherd in the shop across the road from the post office once weighed out a pound of sugar over- instead of under-weight and gave the wrong change – in the customer's favour – when Lily's song came crossing the road (and people regarded Mr Shepherd's behaviour as a greater miracle than that of the duppies!). When Lily sang at night, trees crowded nearer to the house to hear her (being careful to move back by morning), and the soursops and mangoes ripened faster and, one night (you might find this hard to believe), one night an Ol'Higue was getting ready to shed her skin so she could fly off to suck a baby's blood, and at that moment Lily's song came passing by and Ol'Higue's skin started to shiver so much at the sound it refused to leave her, clung to her tightly so Ol'Higue couldn't get out of her skin and fly that night. O the magical things that happened when Lily sang!

Aunt Mercy knew that the young men hung around the post office just to see Lily, so she never put Lily out front to serve the customers if she could help it. She made Lily sit where only the tips of her shoes and part of her skirt could be seen from the window. (And the young men still found that provocative!) Lily sorted the mail, wrote things down in ledgers and dealt with the telegraph system which always confused Aunt Mercy. Lily didn't mind, she was so very happy, her hands were light as high notes. When she hit the telegraph keys her life hummed all the way down the line to her message's destination and back up again. When she stamped letters her touch was so delicate you hardly heard a sound. If she did handle the customers she greeted them most charmingly and read their letters to them quietly in a corner where no one else could hear, whispered them even, and made no comment, nor lectured them about the contents and embarrassed them as Aunt Mercy sometimes did. And Lily laughed at the young men who were in love with her (but not to their faces for she was also kind), especially Mr Abbott the baritone with whom she sang, and who was a man of substance (forty acres, a horse and buggy) and from a respectable family (otherwise Aunt Mercy would never have allowed them to sing together) and who wished to marry her. But Mr Abbott, though nice, was short and *plodding*, Lily found. She didn't want to hurt him so she was gently turning his interest in the direct of Turah who was not beautiful and not terribly bright, but whose family had a lot of land and who was described as rich and who loved Mr Abbott dearly.

Lily paid no attention to the village boys she had grown up with because Lily was young (just seventeen) and felt she had her whole life ahead of her. Lily hadn't been exposed much (beyond the church socials and musical evenings) but Lily was well-read. She had consumed all of Aunt Mercy's library (*In Durance Vile*, *A Maiden All Forlorn*, *Lady Verne's Flight* by Mrs Hungerford) and all of Miss Delevante's (Ouida's *Ariadne*, *Moths* and *Friendship* were favourites) and all of Teacher's Wife's (*she* preferred Mrs Alexander's romances). This was unfortunate since Lily was romantic even without the literature and shared many confidences with her girlfriends, Amy and Jasmine, on the back verandah facing the river when the post office was closed (whispered because Aunt Mercy listened in on everything), and they agreed that there could be only one possible destiny for Lily which was that one day this tall, dark, handsome stranger would come riding by, come ask for Lily, come take her away (where, they were not yet sure) to live happily ever after. Lily knew this would happen with such certainty that this secret knowledge sustained her happiness day in, day out. She hummed as she worked and the telegraph lines hummed too as they took her messages to the world that she was waiting and waiting and she hummed as she stamped the letters lightly as kisses, imagining that every one was to or from her waiting lover, her Prince Charming. . . .

So Lily was not surprised when he rode into the post office compound one day, on a bay horse as she had imagined, and he was tall and handsome with a lovely waxed moustache and elegant clothes and deep, penetrating eyes that raked Lily so hard she felt instant pain. So hard that she almost forgot to greet Mr Dalrymple, the post office supervisor for the parish, an old friend of Aunt Mercy's and almost like a father to her, and he introduced this gentleman Mr Pym from P&T headquarters, doing a tour of the island to write a report of facilities.

But Lily didn't believe for one minute that he was really from P&T, though she admired the strategy he had used to come and meet her. And from the moment his hand touched hers Lily truly honestly could remember nothing of the rest of the day, the night, the next morning when he rode off in a mist after promising to love, honour, cherish her for the rest of their lives. To return, shortly, to break the news to Aunt Mercy, to take her away . . . completely forgetting what happened there behind the big rock at the river that night, completely forgetting about sneaking out of Aunt Mercy's house (the first time she had done so) to wait for Mr Pym (Harold to her), putting it out of her mind completely in her misery at not hearing from him although a few months later it all came back terrifying real when Aunt Mercy, worried about her, how thin and nervous she had become, how dark the circles under her eyes, had taken her to Dr Dampier in Mandeville and he confirmed that Lily was pregnant.

Pregnant? How could that be? For Lily hadn't the faintest idea of cause and effect since no one had told her the facts of life.

Aunt Mercy's reaction was totally lost on Lily for all that mattered was that he had gone without a word, had not replied to the letters she sent him from the post office endlessly, thickly bunched as clouds; she'd heard nothing, nothing. At first she could not believe it, fantasised about accidents, amnesia, his being recalled to England to be knighted by the King and finally after Lily had had no word and was going mad, she did something unthinkable, criminal even. She sabotaged in a crude and childish way the telegraph system so that Mr Dalrymple would have to come and put it right and she could thus get news of Mr Pym (selfishly cutting the village off from the rest of the universe and worse, destroying HM Government Property – a £5 fine!).

When Mr Dalrymple came he did not see Lily, who was indisposed and lying in the darkness of her room, but she leaned her forehead against the painted wooden wall that divided her room from the parlour and heard Aunt Mercy ask (quite casually) what had happened to that nice Mr Pym. Mr Dalrymple said that Mr Pym had had a big promotion in the colonial service and had been sent to the Andaman Islands to reorganise their postal system there. Aunt Mercy was mystified as she had never heard of the Andaman Islands and Lily never heard where Mr Dalrymple said they were located (if he ever said). For she had flown to her school Atlas and couldn't even find it in the gazetteer (though in truth it was a small Atlas and not everything could be included, surely) but how could someone be promoted out of one's life to a place people had never even heard of? And she thought for the first time as she sat listlessly leafing through the Atlas of Mr Pym who had such freedom to stay or to go just like that to the ends of the earth while she, she would always remain here hemmed in by mountains linked only by the hum of the telegraph wires, deflowered, trampled, defiled, besmirched, soiled (for the vocabulary of her reading remained).

For the first time in her life Lily looked at herself, at her body, her brown hands, and though her skin was lighter than Mr Abbott's or her friends Amy and Jasmine's, than most people's in the village, and though her hair was so long and thick it could be piled up respectably on her head with virtually no padding, for the first time in her life she realised that there were other, superior, attributes which resided in whiter skin, straighter hair. In belonging, not to a poverty-stricken little colony, but to Mother England where the King resided. That in the world in which she lived these attributes, these alone, conferred power and freedom.

And she no longer felt beautiful, sharp and crisp with clean edges ready to slice through life but dirty, smudged, second-rate. Unlike Mr Pym, she couldn't do as she pleased, fly out of reach of responsibility, fly from trouble, fly to a new life elsewhere. She was mired in a little village in a little island that Andaman Islanders had never heard of, as stuck in the mud and dirt as Eglantine who had twelve children for eight different men, as Myrtella who had had seventeen (thirteen dead) or Gem and her brood with not a one to mind them, all the women she, all the respectable girls, had once so despised, now she was as fallen as they were. And at that moment she couldn't figure out precisely whether she was suffering like this because she was a woman or because her skin was not white like Mr Pym's.

Now she hated to go into the post office for she couldn't stand the hum of the telegraph wires, the clatter of the keys and when (after it was all over) she came back, for what else was there to do, her fingers were like lead on the keys, the wires never sang any more when she stamped letters, her hand was as heavy as Aunt Mercy's 'THUMP THUMP-THUMP THUMP', she never smiled at the customers and was sometimes rude when they asked her to read their letters, told them to come back even when she was doing nothing and was becoming every day more and more like Aunt Mercy. The worst thing was that Lily stopped singing. Lily never sang again though the young men kept hovering around hoping to hear her. But Lily's song never came and after a while, they drifted off to other homes where the girls were more congenial. In the evenings now the space outside the post office stayed blank and enigmatic and Lily liked it so, for it affirmed that the Lily that she had been, the young innocent girl, the beautiful singer, no longer existed.

The older people were not as mystified by the sudden change in Lily. Because Lily was such a good girl, and Aunt Mercy such a hawk watching over her, no one, not even the worst gossip, suspected the real reason for Lily's illness for they didn't have to look that far. They had seen cases like Lily's before – singing happily one day, wasted by mysterious illness the next. When Aunt Mercy sent Lily away to stay with her sister Mrs DaSilva who was expecting and needed company and left her there for several months, the more knowing understood that Aunt Mercy had done it to get Lily away from the evil forces sapping her life. For shortly after Lily left, that Turah married that Mr Abbott whom everybody knew was so sweet on Lily they would have made such a fine couple and everybody knew that that Turah's people dabbled in spirits. How else could they have acquired all that land they had in such a short space of time? It was clear that that Turah and her family had obeahed Lily so that Turah could get Mr Abbott, who was the best catch for miles around. And everybody secretly gave Aunt Mercy advice on who was the best obeahman to consult to get the spirit taken off Lily (and *thrown back* on that Turah and her family, they strongly advised). And Aunt Mercy, who gossiped about everybody's business but never revealed her own, accepted their sympathies and smiled thinly, saying *yes yes true true* to everything. And made her own plans for Lily.

My Dearest Aunt Dawn,

I hope this letter finds you in the best of health. Sister Lucy and Mr DaSilva likewise. I have not heard from Lucy for ages but I know she is busy with her Harvest Festival coming up and everything. Well, my dear Aunt, I write to you with a *heavy heart* on a matter I never thought in my *wildest dreams* I would have to deal with. But Auntie, not to beat about the bush, Lily is in the *family way*!! Can you believe it? After all the care and attention I gave her from the very day her mother died and left her an orphan. (You know only too well the story of her father if he can be called that.) Believe me, Aunt Dawn, I wanted to kill her. The hardest part is *there is no one here I can breathe a word to*! Now I understand what you and Mama and Aunt Vera went through when Lucy had her 'accident' (?), but of course Lucy has always been lucky and has risen above all that. *Some of us have our bread well buttered!!!* Poor Lily is a shadow of her former self, fretting and fretting. I am trying not to be too hard on her though *she's broken my heart* and every day I have to deal with the public with a smile, as if nothing has happened, and you know more than anyone else *what other heartbreak* I have had in my life. I blame myself, though God knows I kept the most careful watch over Lily except for the *wolf* that actually *came in sheep's clothing*. Totally deceived me. But no matter. Lily is still a good girl who's had her head turned by an unscrupulous calculating man (*as happens to the best of us*).

Auntie, the only good thing is that the father is not one of the common people around or I would never be able to hold up my head. He's a very handsome Englishman with a *big job* in the colonial P&T. Not a little nobody so I guess we should be glad for small mercies. But my dear, he packed his bags and left the country shortly after it happened. So there's *nothing to be expected* from *that quarter.* In any event you know the history of these white men and our women. They might plough and scatter but they do not practise husbandry (as Papa used to say).

My first thought was to marry Lily off to *somebody*. There's a nice young man here who's sweet on her, one of Dan Abbott's boys. Beautiful voice and quite respectable if you remember the family, though a little dark and *hair not the best*. But Lily will have none of it. I hope she doesn't end up *hating all men*, for that happens, *I know*, and though you see her there as such a meek, obedient little thing, underneath she has her grandmother Elie's will and once she has made up her mind *there is no moving her*.

But my dear Aunt, can you imagine my disappointment? No one to turn to but you. Can you talk to Lucy and see what you can do? I'm afraid to write to Lucy directly for the letter might fall into Mr DaSilva's hands and I know how jealous he is. Do you think Lucy would take Lily to stay with her until the baby is born? Aunt Dawn, *I have to get her out of here*. Apart from the fact that Lily's made this one mistake (*paying dearly too!*) not one of us is above reproach and I don't want to ruin her chances for life. Lucy came out of her trouble well, didn't she? Do you think you could work on Lucy to take the baby since she can't have one (*God* forgive her!). She's not too old. In this modern age women are having babies up to a ripe old age and Lucy's not yet thirty.

Anyway, Aunt Dawn, I believe I have given you the picture. I leave *everything* in *your capable* and *blessed* hands. Please write immediately. *I am going mad* with anxiety. Just say the word and I will send Lily.

Your affectionate niece
Mercedes

PS I have written this letter *with such a heavy heart* I have not enquired properly about your dear self. I know you are still getting up at all hours to deliver babies every which way. *What a blessed woman you are*. More than a mother to Lucy and me, to everyone. Please be more than a mother now to our darling sad and very unfortunate little Lily. MN

PPS Make sure to tell Lucy that the *father* (scoundrel that he is), is a very handsome *Englishman*, so Lily with her good looks is bound to have the most beautiful baby in the world and *white* too. I hope it is a *boy* for girl children have such a hard lot in life. Look at Lily, Lucy, all of us. As soon as a boy is old enough he can get on his horse and ride away and nobody says anything but the girls are the ones left behind to carry the burdens. MN

Ah Liberated Man

MARVIN E. WILLIAMS

Foreday morning the other Saturday, Manjack rise up like some insomniac sun and come hollering through mey flaps: 'You ready or what?' I had want to blast his backside to Pakistan or someplace else where Naipaul say need ah energetic sun, but this damn poetry I practising does teach poets to curse underneath their breath so I whisper: 'I coming, man.'

I didn't want to wake up the wife so I there in the dark trying to move quiet-quiet, but I only kicking down radio and rum bottle and so. Tis ah good thing Jojo does sleep hard, because Manjack, the jackass, you think he understand mey situation and shut up? Not he. He only firing blows in the fencepost with ah piece of two-by-four and shouting: 'Man, you ain't ready yet! The fish them gon stop running soon!' I say to meyself: 'Lawd, these bachelor ain't got no heart atall.'

So I hurrying like hell to get out the house, putting right foot shoe on wrong foot, hoping the floor board don't creak and the wife won't get up to harass mey head about taking she to Barker's to buy no girdle for Mespel wedding. Mespel is Jojo first cousin on her father side, and since this wedding to that long-tall Hess man from Aruba announce Jojo got mey running ah limousine service for Mespel. All I hearing is 'Honey, Mespel say she want this from Superfoods' or 'Darling, Mespel want to know if you could drop her by Merchants Market to pick up some meat for the wedding. I tell her that you gon pick her up around seven-thirty.' And if I decide to discreetly mention that that Hess man Mespel marrieding does drive ah brand new BMW, she does get ah attitude what would frighten the devil. The point is Jojo should learn to drive. But no, she too nervous and she ain't paying no taxi when

SHE got ah car. Lawd help mey when her sister from Tobago come to visit we.

Ah drumming start up and Jojo roll over, groaning like somebody hit her. I panic. Manjack with his stupidness there singing 'Barna Jam' off key and driving lick in the fencepost what I just put up last week. Every wrong note he hit, ten twelve dog howl their disapproval like they was a pack of music teachers or something. Jojo call mey name and I jump. I say 'Sweetheart, you call mey?' She smile but she ain't answer. I take ah deep breath and say good. She was only talking in her sleep. 'Small barna, big barna . . .'. I creep out the room and fly out the house and wring the two-by-four out Manjack hand. But it look like he been in ah mood to aggravate me because he break into 'Cockstand' without losing ah breath. I had to stop he in he tracks.

'Manjack, your head good or what?'

'It good like what.'

'I ain't joking, you know.'

'I just feel like singing, man. What wrong with that, eh?'

'Nothing ain't wrong with singing, but you can't wait til the sun come up, man? And if you gotto sing, you must do it so loud?'

'Calypso supposed to be sing loud.'

'But you can't at least sing ah calypso that all these dog around the place ain't know enough to howl along with?'

'They howling in tune, eh? These dog is island dog, man. They got calypso in their blood. Listen to this . . .'.

'Knock it off before you start, you hear me! Knock it off right now before me and you fall out over stupidness.'

'What wrong with you, Soursop? Since when you ain't like to hear calypso?'

'Nothing ain't wrong with me, and calypso should be left to calypsonians.'

'But you yourself say I gotta heapa potential to make calypso.'

'I was drunk when I say that. Look, tis wake up you trying to wake up mey wife and the rest of the neighbourhood, no?'

'You ain't worry about no neighbourhood; you worry bout your wife waking up. She got you under wraps, bwoy. You need to get liberated, man.'

'Let we go, you hear. Tis you say you want to go catch fish, you know. If you stay here and keep hitting them wrong note you dey calling calypso and wake up Jojo we ain't going fishing. At least not me.'

'You ain't tired letting that woman boss you around, man?'

'Ain't ah matter of she bossing me; tis just that she want mey to help her do some things today and I really ain't dey in the mood for it. But if she catch mey, of course, mey mood have to undergo ah radical change.'

'You is ah man or ah mouse? Chupse.'

'When you married the two of them is the same thing.'

'I believe in what Sparrow say: "Be ah man and not ah mouse; put some pepper in she souse; show that louse who is boss in the house." Bam braga, dam. That's calypso!'

'That's calypso for bachelor to hear. Besides I ain't got Papa Jack problem.'

'Man, you know what I mean. The thing is, married or not, no woman ain't bossing me. I gon wear the pants in my house.'

'Woman does wear pants these days too, you know. Tain't like long ago. You ain't notice?'

'The only thing I notice is that the man-mouse them ain't like the man them from long ago. Evolution backwards. My father, man, that was man! Marmy was mey mother name and when he say Marmy jump Marmy hit the trampoline. I gon carry on that tradition.'

'Man always been mouse when it come to woman. They only play rat when they around other man. You know the difference? Long ago woman used to laugh behind man back and call he mouse; nowadays they does call we heapa pack rat mouse to our face. Wise up.'

'No woman could ever call me ah mouse. Tis this damn American television what corrupting woman down here. Let any woman play *young and restless* with me and I gon send her to *general hospital*. Trust me, I would blue-black her eye. Tis ah liberated man I be.'

'Manjack, you ain't tired chat nonsense? No woman ain't gon call you ah man unless you is mouse enough to let her be a complete human.'

'What that bull junk supposed to mean?'

'It mean ah real man would liberate heself from treating his woman like she inferior.'

'Soursop, since you start playing scholar in you old age, reading book left and right and messing around with them nursery rhyme you does call poetry, you talking pure stupidness.'

'Let we go, man. The sun coming up in another hour or so.'

We get in his breakdown truck and start heading for northside, but Manjack won't leave the topic alone. He spieling about what he would or wouldn't do with this or that woman and I trying mey best to tolerate he because I believe the rumours that Manjack never had ah woman in he life and that's why he singing so loud about putting woman in their place and if you hear he talk you would think he was ah real saga bwoy or something who got woman hand over fist and who got them train good-good like them white people dog what does eat steak for dinner and even got their own bed and thing but Manjack ain't got ah nail woman-wise and it strange because he good-looking and everything and he got ah good foreman job with Public Works and plenty woman like he.

'Them Rastaman got the right idea, bwoy. Woman is to procreate and cook food from ground provision. Not give backchat and orders. No siree. Ah woman is supposed to support her man and see that he happy in the sight of Jah. If I wasn't so old I woulda been ah Rastaman.'

'If you wasn't ah old jackass you woulda been ah young jackass.'

'Soursop, you really brainwash for true. What you trying to prove, you is the original sensitive man? Sometimes I does have to stop and wonder if you is the same sweet Soursop who used to be ah proper gable around this island with woman falling all over you and you only saying "Get up and have pride in yourself" while you dey thiefing their pride and more. I does really have to stop and wonder sometimes for true. What happen to you, Sop? Jojo make you sour, no?'

'Jojo help me to correct mey errors.'

'No woman could correct mey error them.'

I was getting sick of these macho thing but I try to keep mey cool, because tis just so Manjack going on and on for the whole ride to Ham's Bluff, during the fishing, and while we riding back with the nine, ten yellow-tail snapper we catch. I just try to ignore he and enjoy the afternoon breeze. I love to feel the breeze as it wafts (maybe gambols more accurate, but wafts could pass) through the trees when the sun go down; especially so when tis ah weekend and I could really relax because I know that it ain't got no work the next day. The breeze does come off the sea fresh and tingling your hot skin if you near enough to the bayside to feel it. And when you feel it, if you smitten by the muse you mad to compose something like ah ode to the tradewind. After that headaching sun we bless with leave we for the day, it does come like even the sea breeze glad it gone, even the sea breeze glad night coming. But

I like the soft wind of morning even better. And though I trying to enjoy the breeze now, Manjack continuing he spouting and I can't avoid his spit.

And to make bad matters worse, when we finally pull up in front mey house around three o'clock that afternoon Jojo dey waiting patiently in the doorway with her hands on her hips. Manjack start to laugh like it going out ah style and I say to meyself: 'Oh Gawd, Jojo, not now. Not in front this idiot.' But when I ease out the truck preparing meyself for the worse I get ah shock. Jojo bounce down the steps with ah big smile on her face. Manjack stop laughing in two-twos, but he manage to whisper: 'Don't let that smile fool you, bwoy; tis licks coming.' I wasn't worry bout licks because Jojo ain't in to hitting mey, but I had ah feeling that curse like rain was waiting in her smile although it was clear not cloudy.

'Soursop, darling, how much fish you catch?'

The question had sound fishy, but I stammer: 'Bout . . . bout ten yellow-tail snap . . . snapper. Nothing else wasn't bit . . . biting and you love yellow-tail anyway.' I is ah man who don't usually stammer, you know, and Manjack pick this up and start to cough.

'Let mey see them, no.'

'They ain't too big, you know Jojo.'

'Oh Lawd! They lovely yes. How much is ours?'

'Half.'

'I gon clean them and cook them up right away. When you wash off and get settle come help mey turn the fungy.'

In the meantime Manjack dey singing 'Licks in the Police Van' over and over and acting like the song ain't have no relevance to mey present situation. Jojo was walking away with the five fish, and halfway up the steps it look like she see Manjack for the first time.

'Eh-eh. Manjack, I forget you been there. How you do, man?'

'I can't complain, Jojo, I can't complain atall. I dey good. I dey good and free as ah bird.'

I whisper to meyself: 'Ah idiot-bird.'

'Well it good that you so free because it have somebody inside I want you to meet. Soursop, I want you to meet her too.'

Manjack start hemming and hawing and mumbling about how tis only when ah man tired everybody does want he to meet people when they know full well that ah tired man don't make good company and besides that ah man would rather not be introduce to no woman when he got on this heapa old clothes and stink ah fish and maybe Jojo could see clear to tell her company that he gon meet her later seeing as how he indispose at the moment and he hope that she enjoy her visit whoever she is and if she still around for awhile then perhaps maybe he might drop by and say hello although she shouldn't really take that as ah promise because he is a busy man who ain't like idleness and got heapa thing to do to keep hisself occupy fruitfully. And he start up the truck engine.

I say, 'Man, Manjack, turn off the engine and get out the truck. You know you ain't got ah damn thing to do. And what stupidness you talking about the clothes you got on too old for introductions? Only old clothes you does wear.' But I meyself was curious about this woman Jojo so anxious for we to meet. And then it hit mey. No wonder she so cool about this fishing business. Her sister come. That's what it tis. But I thought Jojo say she was coming next weekend. But it gotto be her sister Josie. Who else it could be?

'Stop your stupidness Manjack.' That's Jojo talking. 'She really want to meet you. And she understand you been fishing so that ain't no problem. Bring he in, Soursop. I going to tend to the fish.'

Manjack turn off the engine but he won't take the key out the ignition. He lean back in the seat with this worry look on he face, and although he was trying he best to grin like nothing in the world ain't bothering he, I could see that he was uneasy like hell. I make ah mistake and ask if he ain't coming.

'Man, you can't wait? Ah man just trying to cool out and you acting like a Russian. You should pay more attention to the old saying them. You never hear "Don't rush the brush you might get daub"? I ain't like people rush me, you know; it does get me well ignorant, you see mey ya. Just for that I got ah good mind not to leave this truck until I reach mey own yard. Everybody too damn hurry nowadays; that's the problem with this world. Everybody running like wild ants and ain't have no particular place to go. Now, you can't wait!'

'I sorry, man. I see how ignorant it does get you for true.'

'That's supposed to be funny?'

'Look, man, let we go in. I sure the woman is Jojo sister Josie from Tobago.'

'Tobago? I didn't know Jojo was from Tobago. She don't have no accent or nothing.'

'Yes, man. Jojo from Tobago but she been on St Croix from small. I see a lot of picture of Josie and she pretty too bad. You coming or what?'

'I coming, man. I coming. Bwoy, you more Russian than dead Khrushchev.'

'You look like you want to stay in that truck until you dead like Khrushchev.'

Manjack pull the key out the ignition and ease out the truck like it had hand grenade or glass bottle in mey yard. And once he foot touch ground he start patting down what lil bit of hair he have and pushing he old shirt down in he old pants and asking me how he look and getting upset because I smile when I say good and he just was looking nervous-nervous in general so I tell he to take it easy because the woman ain't plan to judge he like he was in some kind of beauty contest. He say I should just shut up and let he make heself presentable so I shut up and watch he get heself presentable and when he done do nothing we head up the steps to the house.

When we get inside I darn near drop down dead. It had suitcase and trunk and hand bag and basket and clothes bag like sand in the living room. It look like ah family of ten had come to visit we. I scratch mey head and search mey mind trying to remember if Jojo had ever tell me that Josie was planning to stay for more than one week. She didn't tell me no such thing. I was just about to call Jojo from out back in the yard where she been cleaning the fish when Josie waltz in the living room from the kitchen. When I say 'waltz' I mean 'waltz'; I ain't just spouting Crucian Creole slang. She waltz as in dance when she come in that room. Manjack see her and stagger, and as if to justify he staggering, he lean over to me and whisper: 'Let we fire some rum.' I tell he let we get pass the introductions first.

'Josie – I recognise you from your picture them – Josie, I is Soursop and this mey old friend Manjack.'

'Old is just ah figure of speech, of course.' Manjack glare at me when he say that, and I was ah lil shock to see mey bwoy so quick on the tongue.

Josie laugh. 'Glad to meet you at last, Soursop. Jojo write and tell me so much good thing about you. You sound like you is ah very good man. Manjack, I very happy to meet you.'

'You ain't happier than me . . . I mean I glad to meet you, too.' And embarrass like the devil, he whisper desperate-desperate: 'Why you don't get the damn rum!'

'Take it easy, man. Take it easy.'

Josie must be see how nervous Manjack was because she keep eyeing he and smiling like she really want to burst out laughing. This time so Manjack sweating and wringing up he hand them like the two of them have in water and he trying to get them dry. I try to break the tension for his sake.

'So, Josie, you look good, man. How long you planning to stay with we? I give you ah week before you start bawling for Tobago.'

'I come to stay for good . . . if everything work out.'

'Come to stay for good?' I could of hardly believe mey ears when she say that, and I had believe them even less when Manjack chime in: 'But you ain't hear what the woman say?'

'I hear yes, but tis just that I wasn't expecting it. So where you working and where you plan to stay?'

'Well, I come here on ah Kasha Hotel bond and Jojo say that you would be happy to let me stay here until I find ah place to live.'

I was ready to explode but some woman got ah sixth sense when it come to these kinda thing so Josie croon some sexiness then say: 'Jojo was right for true. You so sweet and nice.' In the meantime Manjack got this big satisfy grin on he face and though Josie crooning soften me up, I still thinking to meyself that lately Jojo making it ah habit of taking advantage of mey good nature and that I need to make ah stand on this issue because ain't no way in the world Josie could fit in this lil piece of house with me, Jojo and the three children them. Jojo ain't ah bad woman and she usually don't take advantage of me or vice-versa. The two of we believe in fairness and none of we does ask the other to do something we won't do ourself. Manjack ain't know ah damn thing what he talking bout when he say Jojo does boss me. Jojo ain't want no man who she could boss and she ain't want no man to boss she. Tis equality I talking bout and tis equality we got. But like I thinking to meyself now, lately she look like she taking advantage of mey good nature. Yet I find meyself saying: 'Of course you could stay with we til you get on your foot.' The hug she give mey was nice.

'I need ah drink. Manjack, you still want to fire some rum?'

'Man, get the bottle, no man.' He had sound like he been in pain.

'All you keep one another company. I coming right back.'

I wink at Manjack as I was leaving the room and I was surprise to see that the said same man who was just talking big big and out of turn was now shivering when he hear that I coming back. Although I couldn't

tell if he was shivering from fright or from anticipation, I had to laugh for true.
 But I ain't laugh long because I really still had the vex over this Josie-staying thing. So I bolt outside to confront Jojo who happily singing while she scaling the fish.
 'Jojo, how come you ain't tell mey that your sister was coming here to stay? I thought we used to communicate.'
 'What?' She spin round like ah pinchy-narny. 'You frighten me, man. What you say?'
 'I say since when you going doing thing behind mey back?'
 'Honey, what you talking bout? What thing I do behind your back?'
 'Invite your sister to stay here when you know we ain't have room enough to sneeze as it tis already.'
 'Soursop, I was as surprise as you when the taxi drop Josie here with that mound ton of luggage. But since she was already here what I coulda do except make what little space we have available to her? She is mey sister, Soursop.'
 I tell her that it ain't make no sense trying to argue with her (because I really ain't had no argument for what she had just say). But when you prepare for argument you gotto argue.
 'I see ah pattern developing lately where you making promise left and right for me. That ain't fair atall, and I want you to know that I ain't gon stand for it. I mean tis fifteen years we married now and this is ah hell of ah time for you to start acting the fool with me. I ain't know what get into you, but I know you better start cleaning up your act post haste because I . . . .'.
 'Ha-ha! Ha-ha-ha! Oh Lawd, Soursop, I ain't mean to laugh but . . . ha-ha. Ha-ha-ha! Oh Lawd, mey belly.'
 'What the hell you laughing for? You hear me say anything funny?'
 'Yes! Ha-ha-heh-heh-ha-haaaaaa! Sorry. Ha-ha-ha. Sorry, man. Ha-ha-heh-heh. Forgive me. Heh-heh.'
 'Ha. Ha. Heh. Heh. I is the one who should say sorry. I had sound like an idiot, eh?'
 'Yes! Ha-ha-haaaaa!'
 'You ain't have to agree with me so strong, man. I love you.'
 'I love you too. Give me ah lil kiss, man. Umm. Thank you.'
 'But how we gon manage this thing, man, Jojo?'
 'Don't worry, honey, we gon manage. I gon tell you the game plan

later. Go entertain your company (ha-ha-ha) and let mey finish cleaning these fish ya.'

'You want ah rum and something? I fixing one for Manjack. Oh, yes. I forget Josie. She does drink?'

'Not ah drop. Anything but alcohol. Yes, honey, you could make ah drink, rum and water. And make sure it strong.'

'Gimme ah minute.'

How ah man gon fight against ah woman like that, eh? Pure stupidness to try. She too fair, logical and loving, man. I mix Jojo her drink and carry the rum and coke in the living man. You shoulda see mey bwoy Manjack. He and Josie was sitting down on the couch and your bwoy had he leg cross and been posing with hand underneath he chin as if to say he is ah cool daddy. And he chatting away about the relative benefits to be derive from the economy of the Virgin Islands and how it have place here like dirt where ah woman as nice looking as Josie could lime and how he would be too happy to take her out on the town being as how he does frequent all the spots and know all the real good band them and is ah budding calypsonian and how he ain't married because it have so much confusing fish in the sea and he meticulous and selective and choosy that's why he ain't bite no bait yet but he ready to bite anytime he find the right fish and if she would like to go out sometime soon let he know because he could see right now that she like to go out and have ah nice time and he ain't less than the same way and stuff like that he chatting Josie down with.

'See the rum ya! Let we go back to the trough!'

'You come back so quick?' Manjack say.

'It only quick because you having fun.' They laugh when I say this, although Manjack had look ah lil embarrass that I see what was going on. So he get up quick-quick and take the bottle from mey hand and start dishing out rum like he is host. He offer Josie MY glass but she say that she didn't want ah drink at the moment. Up to now Manjack still wondering how come I had laugh that day when . . .

So the three of we sit down there chatting and it obvious that Manjack and Josie hit it off. He powdering rum for courage and rapping sweet-sweet and she giggling at mey bwoy joke them and saying every now and then: 'You ain't had enough of that rum, Manjack?' But mey bwoy been feeling good so he was only laughing and telling Josie not to worry because tis man he name and this lil bit of rum we drinking couldn't nearly get he high much less drunk. But he was stone drunk or at least he was drunk and turning to brittle stone.

Josie excuse herself and went to join Jojo who was now in the kitchen cooking the fish. As soon as she leave, Manjack bolt over to where I was sitting in mey rocking chair to harass mey head.

'She nice, eh! You say she is two years younger than Jojo?'

'Yes.'

Bwoy, she ain't look ah minute over twenty-five. 'She solid-solid and pretty. Lawd, Sparrow right for true bout Tobago woman. Nice and round like ah butterball. Soursop, talk the truth, you think she like mey?'

'She crazy about you, man. You can't see how she eyeing you and laughing after your stale joke them?'

'Nothing ain't stale bout my joke them, you hear! As ah matter of fact they kinda fresh. You ain't see how she been blushing? But you right for true, you know. She was laughing like hell. You think she would go out with mey tonight to the quadrille they having down by the Hall?'

'You have to ask her that, man. Don't ask me. And furthermore, you sure you sober enough to carry anybody anyplace?'

'I sober like ah top.'

'And you staggering like one what tired spin too.'

'Who staggering? Soursop, you know I tired drink you under that old table you have in your kitchen. Stop talk stupidness and pour rum, man.'

'Josie ain't look like she too like the fact that you dey drinking so much, you know.'

'Watch mey, I is ah liberated man. Tain't her business how much rum I drink. Pour Cruzan, man!'

'Okay.' He put out he glass and I angle the bottle to pour.

'You really think she worry bout how much I drinking?' He pull away the glass when he ask that and make mey throw some of the rum on the linoleum. 'You see what foolishness you make me do?'

'I just ask you ah simple question, man. You ain't got to go on so.'

'If you is "ah liberated man" you ain't have to worry your head over what Josie think about you drinking.'

'You right. Fling rum in mey cup! But wait, man. She had look kinda funny when we was drinking for true. I had enough rum for now, man. I gon drink ah lil bit after we eat dinner.'

'You staying for dinner then?'

'You deaf or what?'

So Manjack stay for dinner and we kill fry fish and fungy and he give his portion of the catch to Josie because he say he could see that she like yellow-tail snapper too bad and by the way since she been lock up in the house all day he would like to take her to the quadrille dance where he could teach her all the dance step them. She said yes she want to go to the dance and that begin ah hot romance between Josie and Manjack. They become the talk of the island, and when Mespel married her Hess man Manjack and Josie get more jealous stare than the bride and groom.

And ever since Manjack get in with Josie he come ah new man. He trade in he old truck for ah secondhand Mustang convertible and give it ah good body job so that it had look almost new. And your bwoy only cruising round town with the top down and with one hand on the steering wheel and the other one hanging out the car as if to say he dread-dread and he too much of ah expert to worry about using his two hand them. And although driving with one hand ain't too bad, the thing is Josie dey home-up home-up under the one hand that he have on the steering wheel and you have to wonder how your bwoy does manage to manoeuvre the vehicle. And this affair reach ah point where you don't see Manjack cruising the town without Josie tight-tight against he arm and the two of them laughing and carrying on like teenagers.

This love affair even bring about ah change in Manjack decorum. Every day now your bwoy running home after work and dressing up in he Sunday best. And every day tis ah new outfit Manjack wearing. I self didn't know he had so much clothes. But tain't clothes alone I talking bout. Manjack start walking round with ah afro comb in he back pocket and all-time watching in the rearview mirror and combing he hair or patting it down. And if he ain't doing that, then he brushing dust off he shoes or picking lint off he pants. And he only walking straight-up straight-up like he is ah English butler or something and now and then he talking proper like he is one of them butler for sure. I telling you, ever since Manjack get in with Josie he come ah new man.

But in ah way Manjack ain't really change atall, because after weeks of liming with Josie he still talking big about how woman must follow his programme else he ain't want no part of them. And although I didn't expect ah woman like Josie to allow such ah attitude, I notice that she going along with the programme and looking like she really happy with it. (Who could explain love, eh?) And Manjack really was showing her ah good time for true. Everyday around six-thirty he coming like ah whirlwind and sweeping Josie up and taking her out for dinner or to the movies or to dinner and dance. And when he bring her back home it come like he don't want to say good night. He does always follow her inside and sweet talk her til she beg he to go because it getting late and this ain't her house. But tis only after Josie tell he six, seven times that it late and he have to go that Manjack does kiss her good night reluctantly then leave whistling like ah lark.

The more date Manjack and Josie had the more he had want to get her to come live with he. Every time he come to visit he pulling me aside and asking something not too subtle like, 'This house ain't too small for all all-you?' or 'All-you must be butting up in one another straight' or 'How is the crab hole treating you since I been ya last time?' or something like that what make it obvious what he scheming mind thinking.

And although traffic in the house heavy for true, me and Jojo had get use to having Josie around and we wasn't in no hurry to see her go. So anytime Manjack start up he hinting with 'Sardine in ah can got more room than . . .'. I does say: 'Don't worry your head, man. The sardine them in this can happy too bad.' But that don't stop mey bwoy although it does detour he ah lil bit from he destination. So he does play he slick saying 'Let we fire some Cruzan, man. I notice that you acting stingy-stingy with the liquor these days. What it tis? Jojo take the bottle from you, no?'

And this time so I playing like I ain't know what he up to and giving he the rum and talking baseball and thing. But after two three drink he dey back on course; 'I notice that the whole family don't sit down at the table together to eat no more', or 'My house got room knocking dog.' If I is in ah good mood I does tell he, if he want the woman to live with he then he should married her. But when I in ah bad mood I does tell he to mind he own business because this house is mine and small as it tis we could manage good.

After about three months of this heapa dating and hinting mey bwoy start coming to me with ah new tune.

'Josie is ah woman, bwoy. She sweet too bad. And she know how to make ah man happy without forgetting her place. When I say jump she flying. When I say sit tis lying down she lying. When I say shut up she does ask til when. When I say I is man she does say I is men. (Oh Gawd, I should write that down.) Yes, man, she is ah perfect woman for mey. What you think, Soursop?'

'I think she very nice, but I don't believe she's the kinda woman who could stand for all this bossing around you talking bout.'

'Your problem is that you like to spoil woman. Watch how Jojo does have her own way. I is ah liberated man, bwoy! Josie know that and she respect herself when it come to me. You dey minding them book you does read bout woman liberation and thing. What that book you show mey the other day name? *The New Improved Man?* Chupse. This old . . . mature man ain't need no improving. Them book don't teach you nothing but how to be ah good man-mouse. You better throw away them book and liberate yourself.'

'I is as liberated as I want to get. Don't worry bout me.'

'I ain't worry bout you; I sorry for you. Yes, bwoy. Josie is the kinda woman ah man should married if he want to live happy.'

'Go on and married her then.'

Every time the topic progress to this point he does start hemming and hawing about how ah man should think serious about marriage before he jump into it. Yet from all he saying it was obvious that Manjack seriously ready to jump into marriage but he frighten for some reason or the other. But still he won't leave the topic alone.

'Soursop, you know me good, right?'

'Right.'

'You think I is marrieding material?'

'No.'

'I don't know why I does bother to ask you anything, you know. You ain't tired joke?'

'You ain't tired ask me stupidness?'

'You more experience in these kinda thing than me, so what big thing it tis if I ask you ah few thing, eh?'

'I just sick and tired of your indecision. If you love the woman married her; if you don't then leave her alone. But stop asking mey all kinda bull nonsense, okay?'

'Okay, man, okay. But what you think about marriage in general?'

'Oh Christ!'

Then one day out of the blue Manjack pull mey in ah corner and whisper: 'I want you to be mey best man.'

'Congratulations, man. When is the big day?'
'In three weeks. The first weekend in June. Josie say she had always want to be ah June bride. You think I making the right decision?'
'Manjack, bwoy, I just glad you making ah decision, period.'
'I done got the ring them and thing, everything square away with the church and so, and I keeping the reception at my place. You think it big enough? Of course it big enough, but what you think?'
'I think everything gon be all right, man. Let we go fire some rum. I know you could use ah lil taste.'
'I could use ah big taste, if you really want to know the truth. This wedding business is ah hell of ah thing. You think it too late to call it off?'
'Stop talk craziness, man. Let we go get drunk. It might be your last chance.'
'You think I is you, no?'
'I forget. You is ah liberated man. Ha-ha!'
'You going drinking or you have to go ask for permission first?'
'Let we go, man.'
The wedding went off great although Manjack hesitate couple time when he was repeating the marriage vow them. And the reception was ah real fête. It had people like dirt there; so much people in fact that most of the dancing been in the yard. It had roast goat and rum for spite, and although Manjack had look thirsty-thirsty to join the fellars at the trough Josie had her arm buckle in his own and won't release he until it was time for them to leave on their honeymoon.

They went to Puerto Rico for ah week and as soon as they come back Manjack beat ah hot path for mey house, and before I could ask he how things went he start bawling blood.

'Oh Lawd, Soursop, Josie sweet but she change already, man. She change too bad. Sus Christ, man! I particularly ask you bout married life and your backside only been dey making joke and acting ignorant.'
'Hold on, man. Cool your heels. What you talking bout?'
'I talking bout the fact that Josie blackmail mey love, the fact that Josie lie down next to mey in that hotel in Old San Juan and won't let mey touch her until I agree to all kinda thing.'
'Ha-ha-ha! She do that?'
'You laughing like ah idiot, but this thing serious, man. Woman too damn devious you see them dey. She had mey at her mercy but she wasn't merciful atall. She lie down in a black see-through negligee,

acting sexy-sexy but won't let mey touch her. She won't let mey touch her although I been swearing mey love for her and begging her, sweetheart, to please return to her senses.'

'So what she make you agree to?'

'She say that from now henceforth I was to treat her civil and not presume that I could boss her around because tis woman she be and she ain't plan to put up with that kinda old-time nonsense and if I ever dare try anything like bossing she around again she would show me who is boss. She say she got as much right as any man and the fact of the matter is she ain't approve of her man drinking rum like it was water and moreover if I think I gon be liming every minute with you, I lie, and all kinda craziness like that she make mey agree to. Tis your wife Jojo what put all this lime in her head and make her sour! And although she still sweet in many way, she sour too bad in many other ways I never expect. But the worse thing she plan to do . . . Soursop, I can't tell you why. It private. Heh-heh. The worse thing she have plan for mey is ah pet name. "MOUSIE"! That crazy woman want to call mey "Mousie" in public. You see mey predicament?'

'What predicament?'

Miss Joyce and Bobcat

E. A. MARKHAM

I

Miss Joyce came out on the veranda and sniffed the air and wrinkled up her nose.

'Lord, Lord, have mercy,' she said. 'Why things always work out so? You work, you plan, you prepare; you pay for it with you own money – hard, hard-earned money. But is grudge they grudge. You work and pay, and everything turn out so. I'm too damned soft, that's my trouble. But what's a poor woman to do, a single woman at that? The men have it all their way, the brutes, as always. Bobcat! . . .' Here she shouted at the man in the garden, trying to make herself heard above the sound of the machine. 'Bobcat, you brute. Who paying you to desecrate me so?'

Bobcat, the brute, unaware of Miss Joyce, continued his desecration of Miss Joyce's lawn, digging a hole with an impressive-looking machine.

'We going have to use the back terrace now', Miss Joyce sighed. Then she called to someone out of sight: 'Prudence, we'll have to use the back terrace. I'm sure the grass dying already. Prudence!'

Miss Joyce turned to go back into the house but stopped. Bobcat had seen her but pretended not to. The sound of the machine was not so much deafening as conquering; he was hiding behind that. Now that he was performing for her she didn't know whether to suppress or to encourage thoughts about the nature of the man's machine, the maleness of the thing, the authority of that tool smacking into her lawn, gorging great chunks of soil which left the place so wounded and vulnerable – and the beast, sitting up there on that high seat, like some sort of religion, directing it.

Then Bobcat decided to acknowledge Miss Joyce; he looked up from the still-shuddering machine, the tool suspended in mid-air, and tipped an imaginary hat to her. Miss Joyce refused to be impressed. She wanted the man to know that she was angry, damned angry. She refused to notice the filth that was on the end of the tool.

Bobcat had tipped his hat: who did that sort of thing nowadays? In the old days, when she was a young girl, that sort of thing meant that a man had good manners; then after all the politics and overcoming; after all the raising up of consciousness and women wanting to respect themselves – all that seemed to stop, and only the old-timers were left tipping. Clergymen of the old school, the odd businessman from the country who was thinking perhaps of going into politics. Or the odder fool returning damaged from England. Even the Grammar School boys didn't tip hat anymore. Anyway now was no time, a big woman with so much to do, to be encouraging thoughts about Grammar School boys. And tipping hat was like everything else, just what men did to preen themselves and confuse women.

Miss Joyce started as Prudence silently appeared from the house and stood beside her; she had brought a glass of wine on a tray.

'Don't creep up on me so, you want to kill me? Who ask you to bring out the wine?'

'The cakes ready, Miss Joyce.'

'Prudence, you is a human being.'

'Miss Joyce.'

'Then act like a human being. What you doing with wine in the middle of the day; you want to turn me into a drunkard? Look at the state I'm in already; look at that wild man digging up my front lawn as if it belong to him? Shaking up the house and thing. I getting hot and sweaty again. Do I look ready for a garden party, Prudence?'

'Miss Joyce.'

'I going cancel the whole damn thing.'

'The wine for the gentleman; is he ask for it.'

'Well, that's really good to know. You better go and turn down the oven and don't let the cakes and them burn, eh. So he asking for wine now!' They both stood looking at Bobcat who was enjoying this without appearing to.

'So you all think we running a hotel here? A wine shop? I tell you to offer him a cold drink, and you go and open up the wine put aside for my guests; you know what wine cost in this place?'

'You want me to take it back again?'
'Like the man already move into my home. Ordering this and that. Making demands. Is not just the wine I'm talking about, you know.' And here she shouted at Bobcat: 'So you think this is wine shop? Rum shop?'

Bobcat signalled that he would soon be over, and Miss Joyce said to nobody in particular: 'He can hear. He only playing tricks.' Then she turned again to Prudence. 'Woman, you going let the cakes burn to ashes?'

As Prudence turned to go into the house, Miss Joyce had another thought: 'And you better water the grass, eh?'

'The grass not supposed to water. In the hot sun.'

'Since when you're an expert on grass?'

'Is what they say.'

'Who say? So now you're a Doctor of grass? They give you degree in grass when you was down in the Virgin Islands? That grass come all the way from the nursery. I shame to tell you what it cost.'

'Well, if it dead, don't blame me.' And Prudence went off, unruffled, into the house.

'Is me you all going to kill. I'm only in this world to take a beating.' This time when she called to the man on the lawn, it was with new resolution, and a new name. 'Leslie!'

She signalled and he looked up.

'Stop the damn machine.'

The sudden silence made her a little conscious of her agitation. God, why was it a woman always felt herself in the wrong? The more they abuse you the more you feel guilty. Life unfair, eh?

'Leslie, you nearly finish?'

'Close to.'

'"Close to" not good enough. You promise to come last week.'

'I already explain, Miss Joyce.'

'What good is explanation when I have people coming here in . . .' she looked at her watch '. . . practically anytime now. I'm not a laughing-stock, you know.'

'The smell completely gone now.'

'Maybe the smell nearly gone, but it look bad. In this day and age no one putting in pit latrine in front of they house. I should have built from scratch like everybody else instead of buying from these foreign people.'

'It's the modern thing, you know.'
'They must be addle your brains in London. Since when pit latrine come modern thing?'
'Is septic tank they call it. All the Americans and Canadians put them in.'
'Thanks for the history lesson. Do I look like I in school? I'm not no American and Canadian. I don't have to follow their nastiness.'
'Anyway, you taking out, not putting in.'
'A half-empty bottle look the same like a half-full bottle to them that don't know.'
'You have a way with words, you know? But as I was saying, sometimes, these people, they put them right next to the swimming-pool.'

The man was becoming familiar; she would make him keep his distance, put an end to the conversation. 'This is my front lawn,' she told him. 'No man have the right to pollute it with coarseness, and rudeness and what I call this kind of scatological talk.' Before she disappeared into the house she informed him, in a rather grand manner, that the woman had brought the wine he had ordered.

Bobcat soon collected himself and blew a long whistle in appreciation and tipped his imaginary hat. Not long afterwards, the shudder of his machine could be felt throughout the house.

II

Halfway through the party Miss Joyce, looking cool and unflustered, drifted back to the front terrace to observe the newly-laid turf being watered by a sprinkler. She delayed her re-entry as another guest, an elegantly-dressed young woman, approached the house.

'Celestine, you look nice,' she said. 'Your better half's here ahead of you.'

'Hello, Miss Joyce. You look nice too.'

'Call me Joyce, man.'

'The weather too hot for clothes. I thought you were putting in a pool here.'

'What do I want with pool? I'm not so desperate to let people see me naked. I have two bathrooms in my house, that's enough for me. So child, I'm glad you come. The Very Reverend missing you inside.'

'I doubt that. Papa doesn't believe the cloth should interfere with having a good time.'

'Is Papa you call the Reverend?'

'Got to call him something, Miss Joyce.'

'People might get the wrong idea when you call him Papa.'

'Well, they say he's old enough to be my daddy.'

'People in this place too wicked. Wicked and badminded.'

'Well, as Papa says: we have to show we're not as small as the island. We have to go against the trend.'

'You get punished for that too, child. But what we doing out here talking? Come and join the party. You look nice in truth. The Reverend Doctor must be very good to you.'

A short time later, Celestine was back on the front veranda sobbing in Miss Joyce's arms.

'Brutes, that's what they are. Men are brutes,' Miss Joyce consoled. 'Don't cry, child; they not worth it, none of them. Priest and beggar, all the same. Black and white, no difference.'

Prudence approached from the house with a glass of water on a tray.

'He still playing the fool in there?' Miss Joyce wanted to know. But Prudence remained silent.

'Prudence, you don't hear me talking to you?'

'Is not me invite him here.'

'What's that supposed to mean? Is your family. You all country people together. But it serve me right, I should mix with my own kind.'

'Everybody is family. Me not responsible for that. Reverend Doctor don't change people. Is not me invite him here.'

'I'm sorry I upset your Ladyship.'

'I know him since he small, know how he is. When he use to come up to the big house, Mrs Parkinson old house where I used to work, and that man didn't have nothing, not even a little cardboard suitcase to he name, nothing. And these kind people take he in, buy him clothes. Is me who used to wash them. And he look nice, you know? He always look nice. The boy poor but he could preach even in them days. And they help him along, and they help him along till he marry into the family. And as they help him along he let them down, and as he let them down they forgive he. Every time. And though he married he go and make baby with all kind of dirty, stinking woman. And still they forgive he. And even in the very kitchen, you know where you peeling breadfruit and green banana, he coming in to feel-up you breast.'

Celestine, who had been sobbing all the while, was virtually howling now. So Miss Joyce spoke to Prudence in some anger.

'Woman, you not shame to be talking like that in front of this poor child? Don't no one have any little sensitivity or delicacy in this place?'

But Prudence was unrelenting. 'Excuse my manners. I know what I know. He borrow money and they have to pay it back. He bad, bad, bad. Is preaching save he. Every Sunday when he call the Lord down on we, we frighten, frighten.'

'Jesus God.'

'. . . And when he get into more trouble, they send he away to come preacher. I tell you when Miss Polly marry he I did cry, I cry bitter tears because I know how it go turn out. And they say even to this day he would have other wife and family in foreign country . . .'.

Prudence stopped as the Reverend Doctor appeared in the doorway.

'Ladies, ladies . . .' he hesitated, not sure which one to approach. 'Ladies, excuse my . . . tardiness.' Then he took the glass of water from Prudence. But before taking it to Celestine, he lingered to rebuke Prudence, hardly bothering to lower his voice:

'You never did have any breasts worth talking about.'

III

That evening, after the party, Miss Joyce was sitting on the front terrace, from time to time sipping her drink. She was bothered by a mosquito or a fly and clumsily tried to deal with it. But her mind was elsewhere. She was wondering why she was making a fool of herself. The effort of the party had left her, not drained but agitated. Not even that. Deflated. Why didn't anything ever turn out as planned? When she had lived abroad and couldn't live as she wanted, she had always promised herself that one day it would be different. And she had saved her money. It wasn't easy lifting up racists off their hospital beds to clean them, but she had gritted her teeth and held her breath and done it in the hope that one day she would be able to live again like a human being.

She was aware that there was someone on the lawn, but she was in no hurry. She thought a bit more of what she would or would not suffer in this place. Finally, in her own time, she addressed the shadow on the lawn:

'Bobcat, what are you doing on my lawn this time of night?'

'I come to apologise, Miss Joyce.'

'What for?'

'For missing the party.'

'Too late as usual. Apologies not accepted. Too bad there's no wine in the house. Rum shop close.'

'What can I do, Miss Joyce?'

'I'm not your father and your mother. You can leave my lawn and take your apology with you.'

'Let me explain.'

'I've heard the explanations. Story of my life.'

'May I have a little drink?'

'Never say the woman so stingy she wouldn't even let them come and drink her out of house and home.' She got up to go into the house. 'Maybe I'll be a bartender in the next life.'

Bobcat came out of the shadows and up to the edge of the veranda, but didn't mount the steps. And it was here that Miss Joyce passed over his drink.

She was very calm when she spoke. 'If you want to cross this threshold, Leslie, you have to make me feel like a human being.'

'You're something special, you know, Miss Joyce.'

'Everything on this earth is special. God see to that. Even the crappo you hear waking up the dead is in some way special.'

'No, no. But I mean, really special.'

'You not giving me anything, Bobcat, to call me special.'

'God, you going to be hard to please.'

'You find the foreign ladies easy?'

'I made a mistake, man.'

'You're damn right I'm hard to please. If you have an interest in me you have to find out where I am and meet me there. Is the only thing will compensate for the beating and the punishment.'

'Miss Joyce, you have the wrong man.'

'Every woman in this world have the wrong man. We all have the scars to prove it. But I'm not a child, Leslie, I'm not looking for Mr Right. Over the years, I've learnt the value of compromise. Let's drink to that.'

'Let me come up and sit down, eh. Because I have to talk to you real serious.'

Miss Joyce didn't object. But Bobcat found it hard to start.

'I don't know what you think about anything,' Miss Joyce encouraged.

'Like what?'

'I don't know you, man. You must have views. Views on . . . on the President of France, the Brazilian rain forest . . .'.

'I'm in business, you know, not politics.'

'Oh Leslie, are you a man of imagination or a miser?' She stopped him trying to answer and rushed on: 'Your vocabulary, Leslie: where are the gentle words to . . . make it all better? I expect finesses from a man. I expect something uplifting, not talk about pit latrine and nastiness. I expect reassurance from a man. I want him to tell me that in spite of everything, we not turning into brutes.'

'Everything like what?'

'Oh God. Everything, man. Everything in the world. Violence. Brutishness. Do I have to spell it out? You have to talk to me.'

'Miss Joyce, you're a Philosopher, in truth.'

'When you're up there, high up on your machine, I want to know what you thinking.'

'I like you, you know. That's what I'm thinking. You hear me?'

'That's a cool way to say something. In such a hot climate. You like me like you like rum and cricket?'

'I love you, man.'

'It hurt to say it?'

'Joyce, I love you.'

'That's nice.' Then a little shift in tone. 'You can't imagine that's all a woman want to hear.'

'You going make me make a fool of meself.'

'That's bad? You don't like me enough to risk making fool of youself? Maybe you should send me a letter in a brown envelope. In some other language. In French. M. Bobcat, 48. Bel homme, très sympathique (You have to lie, they all lie), entreprenant, d'un naturel réserve, très sympathique des affaires, etc.'

Bobcat blew another long whistle of appreciation.

'Then maybe I could accept that as a starter,' Miss Joyce said flatly.

'You can toy with a man just so much,' Bobcat threatened, advancing on Miss Joyce. 'I running out of patience, rapidly.'

'So run.'

'I ain't running, Joyce.' His hands were on her.

'So you like me?'

'I love you, man.'

'You like me?'

'Oh God.'
'Ce vrai?'
'Oh God, Oh God.'

PART II

'Dissa Pickney Mean Fi Kill Me'

Mothers, Fathers and Children

Baby

VJANGE HAZLE

The blackness of the night crowded over Gilley; in fact, no one could see the thirteen-year-old figure clad only in khaki pants, without a torch. But no one was about on that black night, no one, that is, except a little boy, his bare feet leading him as his eyes could not, his mother's urgent pleas still echoing in his ears. His mother. Her smooth black face seemed to appear out of the darkness, her voice drowning the sounds of toads and crickets. A loud drumming penetrated his body, carrying him up the hill to Sweetie's house. The black mongrel yelped as Gilley's broad left foot spread heavily on its wire-thin tail. Inside the house Sweetie muttered a curse meant only for the creatures whose sole business was to stalk the night while the world slept.

'Is me, Gilley, Miss Sweetie.'

The door was flung open and a figure clad in white entered the door frame, its white-wrapped head almost touching the top. No questions were asked, the woman acted quickly. No one would come to call Sweetie at this hour unless the moment had come for another life to be assisted into being, and a woman was bawling as agony tore at her gut. Gilley led the way, shading the blazing fire of Sweetie's bottle torch with his sweating hand. They hurried down the unpaved road.

*

The lamp burned feebly in Vena's room. She heard the front door open and close and then Sweetie's whispers to Gilley before her own door opened and the midwife appeared. A sturdy black woman of forty who herself had never experienced the fury of a human infant as it struck out for total freedom. Sweetie had, in twenty of those years, relieved so many women of their vengeance-wreaking bulk that her face had become lined and hardened in sharing the women's distress and in her own childlessness.

'Lawd, Sweetie, ah nevah glad fi see anybody so in all mi life.' Vena's voice was faint, 'Dissa pickney mean fi kill me.'

'Dis quiet yuhself, missis. Afta yuh got five aready, how dissa one fi kill yuh? Yuh well know seh no pickney no dead ina fi mi hand. Jus lay dung an easy as cheese Easton pickney a bawl dung di place.'

Much later Vena lay on the double bed. There was now little evidence of what had taken place earlier, except for the haggard face of Vena and the thin five-and-a-half pound infant sleeping beside her.

*

The night had gone and slivers of sunlight were reaching the two-bedroomed house. Gilley was already up, the sound of machete on wood evidence of that.

'Mornin, Missa Easton. Mama have baby las night.'

The good-looking young man who had entered the yard stood uncertainly for a moment.

'How she be? She get up yet?'

'No sar, ah doan hear no soun from di room yet but Margery gawn mek tea fi har, sar.'

'Wha kinda baby?'

'Me no know, sar.'

Easton hurried up the stone steps into the house, calling Vena's name as he did so, a faint note of elation giving his voice a high-pitched quality. A weak sound was the reply.

'See yuh baby deh, Easton.'

'Vena, yuh aright?'

'Nuh badda bout me, man. Yuh no waan hol yuh gal pickney.'

Easton's face fell. A girl. Oh, Jesus. He had often considered himself the possessor of a strong back and Vena's giving him a male child would have added proof to his boast. Vena already had four boys to four other men's credit.

'Wha kinda coolie gal dis yuh gi me?'

'Yuh nuh know seh a so all baby hair stay when dem born.'

'She not even look like me. Yuh sure seh a fi mi.'

He picked up the bundle. The baby started whimpering. Slowly he put her back beside her mother.

He could barely conceal his disappointment.

'Ah hope she is a bway yuh gi me nex time, yuh know, Vena.'

'A six pickney me got now, Easton, man.'

'Cho Vena, man, yuh know seh is a bway me did want, is a mistake dis. Me mussi did tired, but next time it bound fi be a bway.'

'Easton, kum outa mi room an leave me in peace. Oonu man mus believe seh baby jus come so. Call Margery wid di tea fi me. Lawd, ah feel like ah gwine dead.'

Vena's eyes closed and panic swept over Easton. He rushed to the door.

'Margery, hurry up wid di tea, gal, yuh waan kill yuh ma, nuh.'

Vena's eyes were still closed when he returned to the room and an uneasy feeling started forming inside him. The baby beside her screamed for attention, its spidery legs slowly cutting the air. The door opened and Easton sighed.

'Mama', Margery whispered, placing the rusting tray with its mug of cerasse and plate of mashed potatoes and callaloo on to the ancient wooden dresser.

Easton watched apprehensively as Margery touched her mother's pale dark forehead. He saw when the hand trembled.

'How she so cold?'

The fear was visible in Easton's eyes. The baby was wailing out of the full depths of its lungs.

'Gilley, Gilley, go call Miss Sweetie quick.'

'Wha happen?'

Gilley rushed in, dropping his machete and the piece of wood he had been splitting.

'Mama. It look like she. . . .'

'Look afta di baby an doan tell Septie an Denton dem nuttin.'

Once more Gilley set off for Sweetie's house, the light of day adding speed to his feet. Easton stood staring at the ashen features of the woman who had, a few hours previously, been bringing another life into the world.

'Whey mama deh?' Sonny mumbled, his fore and middle fingers hidden inside his mouth.

'Me nuh done tell yuh aready, man,' Margery said impatiently, 'she gawn a town. She might get work dere.'

'Den how she nevah tell me?'
'Yuh ask too much question. Gallang a yuh bed.'
'Me waan mama.'
The room was cold and quiet as the children sat together on the floor. Gilley's eyes were clouded as he watched his sister trying to do her homework by the light of the lamp.
'Yuh nuh done, yet, Margery,' Sweetie called from Vena's room. 'A time fi oonu go a bed, yuh know.'
'Jus two more, Miss Sweetie.'
'Septie, Denton an Sonny oonu suppose to a draw long buggy by now.'
'Yes, Miss Sweetie.'
The three rose and disappeared into their room.
'Gilley, yuh tink seh mama go dead?'
Gilley thought of the shrunken creature on the hospital bed.
'Dem say is coma. Me nuh know wha name so but dem say she wi come back to because she know she have we to look afta.'
'Suppose dem obeah har?'
'Nuttin nuh name so.'
'Look wha happen to Auntie.'
'Nuttin nuh go so. Dat wicked man Missa Easton not even come look pon we fi say, "Dawg how oonu do".'
The last phrase so reminded him of his mother Gilley closed his eyes and swallowed.
'Yuh no done yet?'
'Me cyaan do dis. Mekki stay, yaah.'
Sleep took a long time to come. It had done so ever since the day Vena had so silently slipped into another world, leaving behind her six offspring in the care of anyone who wished.
Sweetie had wished. She had prayed for the gift of a child. Now, tonight she cradled Vena's infant to her warmth. Go, Vena, go, her mind cried as the baby she had named Precious reached toward her bosom, whimpering. Give me this child, oh God, Vena has done her duty to you. Now I must do mine to you and her. Sweetie's prayer echoed into the night and tears flowed.
With the sunlight came a feeling of satisfaction and she felt at peace as she entered the hospital ward later that evening. Vena's bed was empty, the white sheet stretched tightly across it. The flowers on the table were gone. Sweetie trembled as she walked toward the nurse.

'Oh, Miss Blake is outside. She came out of her coma last night.'

Being wheeled in from the balcony, Vena saw the sickened look on Sweetie's face as she gripped the iron railing of the bed for support. Sweetie couldn't be pregnant, was her first weak thought.

The Occasional Sadhu

RABINDRANATH MAHARAJ

He was in a drugstore; the type that sold senna, lamp-oil, soft candle, fresh aloe leaves and a variety of laxatives and skin creams made from the local weeds that grew wild in every backyard, but in the drugstore were dried, ground and packed loosely in cylindrical bottles about three inches long.

The owner of the drugstore, a man of about forty but looking much older, with the kind of squinting eyes and furrowed face that came from counting and re-counting all the dollar bills and coins before placing them in a cellophane bag, not inside the cash register, but in a drawer beneath the counter, appeared hassled and impatient. That was more than ten years ago but I can still remember the sudden burst of anger.

'Get out. Get out. Look how you driving away all me customers!' Desperation seeped into the anger. He seemed to be helping the man out but I remember that final shove that propelled him out of the door.

The owner told my grandfather, who was affected by high blood-pressure and who had come to purchase some medication, 'I don't know what this place coming to. Every side is vagrant and beggar trying to get what little money you have.'

Through the glass door I saw him holding the coins uselessly with one hand and balancing on the lamp-post with the other. Then he moved off, limping awkwardly.

Later, on our way to the taxi-stand, in a street with stores selling footwear, agricultural implements, old brown magazines and religious pictures, past piles of rubbish and bottles brought down by the drain and lining the pavement, we saw him sitting on an old piece of cardboard, just next to an old woman who looked on with a detached hostility as we approached.

My grandfather, overweight and unable or unwilling to sit, stood over him and I, about fifteen or so, closer to him and sitting on the cardboard; observing the unease as he looked up. He recognised us from the drugstore. I recall thinking that he may have felt embarrassed. I wanted then to tell him that I had seen the money in his hand.

My grandfather sat next to him. I was surprised. He had a rigid code of dignity, brought about by his weight but also I believe, because of the wealth he once possessed and the land that he still owned, all of which limited his range of movement and made him appear to be grim, proper and important.

My grandfather held a green, five-dollar note in his hand. It seemed so simple: like the termination of some business transaction.

The face, brown with streaks of grey beard, remained impassive, then the eyes softened, seemed to acknowledge the act. He shook his head. My grandfather held the money, made a sound as if clearing his throat, then replaced the bill in his shirt-pocket.

The man went into the taxi with us. I cannot remember what exactly was said to him but I recall when the car slowed by the traffic-light, he, perhaps thinking that the unusual act of benevolence had run its course, opened the door and placed his guava-wood walking-stick on the asphalt road. My grandfather, with the merest wisp of amusement, said, 'Wait, wait. We ain't reach yet.' For the entire journey he remained silent and with the wind blowing his long, greyish hair backwards, I thought of how much he looked like those swamis and yogis that my grandfather had often told me stories about, adding his fanciful touch and endowing them with powers and virtues beyond ordinary humans. But when I observed the torn checkered shirt and the frayed khaki trousers, the image seemed discordant and almost blasphemous.

When we arrived, he stood at the entrance to the tent, clutching his small, brown leatherette pouch, the type used by taxi-drivers to keep their money, driving permits and insurance certificates. My grandfather was speaking to my parents and a few of the villagers who had assisted during the last few days. He was a sadhu, my grandfather was saying, and would stay with us for the next seven days.

At that time we were having a religious observance – a Ramayan Yagna – which ran for seven nights during which time there were fragmentary mythological discourses, singing and chanting and then finally, the feeding. Visitors listened, ate, and left. A few, however, seemed affected and moved; they remained after the feeding. I remember thinking, during the preparation, what a waste this was. Bamboo sliced and patterned into elaborate canopies, yards and yards of crêpe paper cut and fashioned into all types of intricate designs, religious pictures hurriedly purchased, others crudely drawn by the village artists; knocking, hammering, tying, fastening, hanging: unending noise and activity. I wondered why all of this was not held in the temple just a mile away. But my father explained that my grandparents wanted this to be held at their residence before they died and I recall being satisfied with that explanation.

My grandfather was saying, 'He will sleep with the other sadhus and them in the corner of the stage.'

My mother seemed worried. 'What kinda sadhu he is, wearing them clothes?'

'Is okay. We will get a dhoti and a merino for him,' my father said.

A simple matter: the appropriate apparel transforming him, in my mother's eyes, from being a useless vagrant to someone religious and pious. It was the type of uncomplicated ritualism that she lived by. And that night, huddling with the other sadhus, he really looked pious and holy. The following morning – I was still tired because I had been awake until after midnight – I was awakened by the voice of one of my uncles.

'Aye man. What you doing they?'

I roused myself and went to the front porch, what we called the gallery.

My uncle was still shouting. 'Aye. Take care you fall down. Leave all that alone.'

I peered down. The man was hobbling about and collecting the pieces of paper on which the religious food – prasad – was served and placing them in an empty rice bag. He seemed not to hear, limping with his guava stick, collecting the paper, straightening the chairs, resting against the bamboo post to catch his breath, then limping off again. When he reached the elevated stage on which the sadhus were still sleeping, he sat and wiped his forehead.

My grandfather said, 'A cripple doing all this while them lazy vagabond and them still sleeping.'

I was surprised. I had never heard him refer to the sadhus in this manner.

When my father went for the rice bag, he waved him away.

This was the pattern for the next few days. During the night he would sit in the corner of the stage next to the temporary bamboo wall, listening to the discourses and the singing, and the following morning he would awaken before anyone else, cleaning, fixing and rearranging. Once or twice my father asked him to discontinue, explaining that there were other persons designated for that work. But he continued. One of my uncles, Shami, said, 'He just repaying a favour.' My grandfather silenced him with harsh words spoken in Hindi; to me it sounded like something obscene.

One day I saw the man looking intently at one of the pictures portraying a Hindu goddess with multiple arms and thought then of his infirmity and wondered how he had arrived at that state. I knew that he was not really a sadhu and this was not because he lacked piety or mystical powers: that earlier image had shifted when I discovered that the silent and impressively impassive demeanour that the sadhus displayed was really a type of involuntary humility. They were, in the eyes of their benefactors, merely objects to be fed, clothed and temporarily housed; anything else was redundant, a position that they seemed to understand. The man's temporary appropriation of the role was largely enforced: the earlier charity, having been denied, limited the other liberal options.

He was standing there, holding his leatherette pouch, resting his slight frame against his walking-stick. A little girl, running, tripped against a protruding chairleg and fell. I saw the walking-stick being levered upright but the girl got up and ran off. He looked at the small, departing figure, then sat on one of the chairs, his head bowed, propped against the stick. Above his head, the wind ruffled the crêpe paper and the gossamery coquillage sprung to life; the gods and goddesses seemed to be flying away.

My mother said, 'It look like he meditating.'

Shami said provokingly, 'Everybody better watch out. Just now he might go in a trance.'

My mother said, 'Why you don't shut up?'

Shami said, 'Why you vex for? He is just a occasional sadhu.'

From the corner of the stage, a very old sadhu – who had not shifted away from his corner since his arrival – was staring at the object of my uncle's amusement with a rigid, unflinching expression. With his eyes fixed, he scratched his head, with long, slow, strokes.

The memory is vivid, like an old, faded photograph. Two old men, one mottled with age and looking like a decaying, neglected, ancient statue and the other not quite fitting into any precise role at that point, other than as a silent sweeper, offering nothing else, not even uttering words, cloistered within his distant secrets.

During the rest of that day – the final day – he tended to the elevated stage – the singhasan – where the pundits and the singers sat, removing the wilted flowers which had been placed in improvised bamboo vases and tied with wires to the posts, wiping away the dust from the fragile styrotex temples that housed the miniature idols, reaching up with his walking-stick and rearranging the mango leaves strung on a nylon twine and criss-crossing the stage.

'First time them god and them getting so much attention,' Shami remarked.

And then the night. I have thought several times of that night and the following morning. Sometimes a memory of half-forgotten things is delineated, made sharper and given focus and depth through some simple incident that cannot be shunted aside or made mutable or malleable, enabling one to choose or discard fragments, to fit the memory itself within an ideal. I believe that was it, not for the final night, the events associated with this occasional sadhu: the sight of his humiliation in the drugstore, sitting on the pavement, clearing and sweeping, all of this would have been lost. And even now I sometimes think that I have inserted pieces of drama into this recollection. But then I know that this is not true, because the events have stiffened in my mind and I see them as if they had occurred yesterday. I see the pundit wiping his face with a saffron cloth, shifting, easing the strain on his knees, relieved perhaps that his week-long task had ended. I see the sadhus and Brahmins seated on the stage, tucking away the money they had been given, somewhere within the folds of their dhotis. I see my father approaching the end of his interminable vote of thanks, speaking about someone who had, in spite of his ailment, ensured that the place was 'clean and pure', and then calling that person to the microphone. And I see the old man reluctantly and awkwardly emerging from the unlit part of the stage, holding a dwarf palmiste palm for support. And then, that moment of uncertainty, when he just stood there, with his head bowed, holding the microphone.

Then he sang his song. The voice, quivering, too high perhaps at first, then settling, smoothing out, arriving at a harmony with the mood of the congregation, being lowered to a fluting whisper, gathering momentum and strength and permeating the hanging decorations, echoing through the bamboo canopies, rising from the burning cedar and incense smoke.

And the religious song – the bhajan – giving energy to the harmonium player swaying and careening over the wooden instrument, to the boy beating the drum, his hands barely visible, to the sadhus and Brahmins, bestirred and watching on with confusion and anxiety.

It may seem simple being written on the pages like this: perhaps a talented singer energising his audience. But there was something else. I had never been enthralled by the mournful or unnecessary harsh bhajans that I had heard at religious occurrences but that night the song took me to ancient crumbling temples, to vines entwined over dusty statues, to a scorching sun and bodies writhing in pain and in pleading, to an unnatural and frenzied joy bubbling and bursting from within all this degradation and despair. To a joy hinged more to a fixed fatalism than to any notion of reality. And then everything becoming inseparable, the hope and the despair, the joy and the suffering. It took me to a past I had not known and to a belief of which I had only seen the fringes.

The following morning I saw him sitting on the edge of the stage, putting on his wooden sapats. His leatherette pouch was fixed beneath his arms. I felt that he was ready to leave and in the lethargic tranquillity that marked the termination of the Ramayan Yagna, his performance the previous night was already half-forgotten. My father, who had awakened early that morning to supervise the removal of the folding chairs which had been rented to us during the week, asked him, 'You leaving?'

From somewhere in the gallery, my grandfather shouted, 'The van didn't come for the chairs yet?'

I answered, 'No, but the sadhu mister who sing last night leaving.'

I heard my mother's voice, 'Tell him to wait. I packing some things in a bag for him.'

My grandfather came down the steps, walking slowly and breathing heavily. He lowered himself on to the stage, 'So you sweep out and clean out already?'

'He up since five o'clock,' my father said.

My grandfather observed the pouch secreted beneath his arm. 'Don't go yet. They packing up a few things for you.'

The man looked disturbed. I saw him removing his pouch from beneath his arm and passing his finger along the zipper.

I asked him, 'So what you have in that case?'

'Go in the back and play,' my grandfather said angrily, words he had used to register his displeasure for as long as I can remember. 'Always playing the fool.'

But I was saved. My mother came with the bag containing clothes, rice, potatoes and perhaps money.

'This is my whole life right here, son. Everything.' The fingers caressed the pouch as if it was a living thing.

It was the first time I heard him speak and I was surprised at the briskness of the voice. I remember seeing a pained, childlike expression flickering briefly and I saw then that he was not as old as I had previously assessed. I saw the finger running irresolutely along the zipper and then I heard the sound of a zipper being pulled. He withdrew a piece of glossy paper and held it towards me. My mother peered over my shoulder. It was a photograph of a young man, laughing, his teeth exposed and a little girl seated on his left leg. She had two bow clips in her hair and she was looking at the photographer with a distraught, rueful half-smile.

'I was about thirty years old then,' he said.

'That is you?' My mother took the photograph from my hand. 'But all this jacket and tie? And who is the little girl?' I saw the muted disbelief on my mother's face. He gave me another photograph. It was of the same little girl, older now, but with the same rueful expression.

'Ooh! Look how pretty she come out', my mother said.

Then: so many questions to ask, so many things removed from formed impressions. I observed the bearded face and tried to formulate some connection with the pictures. My grandfather, looking at the first photograph, said slowly, 'Yes. Is you really. But you looking well-off.' The unstated part of the question lingered. He took out then a brown and folded newspaper clipping. I read. It dealt with a young insurance salesman who had been involved in a vehicular accident and who, after lying unconscious for thirteen days in the hospital, miraculously survived. Other photographs were produced, other letters and accounts, each relating some episode in his life, each in order, and this sequence told me that he had gone over the story of his life – in that little leatherette pouch – several times.

After the accident, he lost the use of his left leg and was unable to work. He began drinking, his earlier life faded, and the periodic memories of that time brought a despairing irritation which could only be displaced by further drinking. And then, he alone, drifting, barely surviving, living on the pavements.

Fifteen years or so at the time, and I recall thinking that his story was unreal and unnatural. Later on, I discovered that in our island, the gap between pavement and power was not so wide, and that far more people than I had previously imagined had made the journey. Loss of fortune, family disputes, diminution of power; all types of reasons – some ridiculously trivial – acting as conduits, and all types of persons making the trip.

I asked him, 'You have no family left?'

He gazed once more at the photograph of the little girl sitting on his leg. 'She . . . this is my daughter.'

'She dead now?'

'No, son. She living somewhere up in Canada.'

'You never try to contact her?' my father asked.

He began to cry. I was glad that I had not asked the question. I looked at my grandfather's face.

My father said, 'Is okay. Is okay. She must be big now.'

He wiped his eyes with his merino. 'Yes, she big now. And she don't want to see me again.'

'And what about your wife?' my mother asked, becoming increasingly intrigued by the story that was unfolding.

'She is all I have,' he said resolutely, tracing his fingers over the picture of the little girl. 'All I have and she don't know whether I living or dead.' After a while he added, 'And she don't care.'

We asked him to stay. My grandfather offered him a job in the ricemill, but he was insistent about leaving. Later, in the inevitable family discussion, my mother said sadly, shaking her head and clacking her tongue, 'He didn't want to get too attach. That is why he had to leave. He living off his loneliness now.' It made sense then and it makes sense now.

Living off his loneliness, polishing his degradation, soothed by both.

I never saw him after that and now I am uncertain as to whether he is dead or still living on the pavements, moving from place to place. But a few days ago I read an article in one of the daily newspapers and I thought of him. The article dealt with a Trinidad-born anthropologist, attached to a Canadian university, who had received an award for some research she recently had done. Next to the article was a picture of the woman, looking assured and poised, barely masking her rueful smile.

Pan for Pockot

LIONEL SEEPAUL

The black fist punched the flour-sack curtain. Then the black, emaciated face was shrieking, 'Stop beating that pan, Pockot. You want to deafen me and Mister Harris? Night and day you playing that Jerusalem song as if you want the saints in heaven to hear you.'

Lady Emelda broke out into coughing. 'This dust giving me asthma.'

From the bedroom, adjoining the kitchen, Mister Harris was also heard to cough. He was a retired engineer, whose meagre pension assured him lodging in this shack of Corbeaux City.

'Pockot,' she called hoarsely, 'just now you has to go to work in the grocery across the city.'

The boy, somewhat tall for sixteen, removed the pan from around his neck, and thrust two sticks tipped with red rubber into his rear pocket.

Lady Emelda quietly marvelled at the creation of her son. Three months ago Pockot was hammering away at the oildrum, brought back from the smoking dump. Squatting before blue-green flames he tapped out day-by-day circles, ellipses, and ovals, upon which from memory he impressed thirty-two distinct notes.

With hammer and punch he dotted the shapes containing the quavers, semi-quavers, and demi-semi-quavers. He was the creator of the Ping Pong, the smallest but sweetest of the other tuned oildrums – the bass, the cello, and the guitar. The schoolmaster was outraged; he flogged the boy for sacrilege, for reproducing those notes of his piano on some rusting pan! Pockot was expelled from the school.

Already he bore a stigma: before his birth Lady Emelda had stabbed the man alleged to be his father.

Yet somehow Lady Emelda had found her son a job in a grocery operated by a Portuguese gentleman, one of her former patrons at the city's Breakfast Shed where she had been a prosperous food-vendor.

'Ah,' she sighed, gazing out at the smouldering dump.

'That day when I see the boy sawing that oildrum in two, I say he was making he poor mammy a washtub. But the boy just like his good-for-nothing father who used to collect free oildrums from British and American ships and sell them to steelband leaders for big profit.'

Mister Harris coughed.

Lady Emelda shouted, 'Boy, go throw 'way these crab-back before they stink up the place. I already late making Mister Harris callalloo'.

Sadly she recalled, 'Is my sins I paying for. But only the Lord know I didn't mean to . . .'.

She saw herself again the prosperous but lonely food-vendor listening to the short stevedore, thumping his thigh with a bar of newsprints. Despite the scars about his face, Lady Emelda had yet found him more pleasing than either Mister Harris or her Portuguese patron.

So, one wet afternoon, she let herself be coaxed down to the wharf. The tide was out. Along the blue-warped carpet of mud, slimy stumps with dark-grey oysters dotted the shoreline. Lady Emelda shivered; the air smelled. Scores of tiny crabs and swollen fish lay lifeless in the mud. The darkening sky with the red blur of sun dipping down behind the blue haze into dark blue waters awed her. She would have turned back but onwards the stevedore had coaxed. Soon the scarlet ibis, those lively, red-plumed birds, would be feeding freely among the mangroves, unaware of squatting tourists taking snapshots of them.

Lady Emelda had groaned aloud. Whorls of sandflies hovered over her. Even the newsprints under her were damp.

Next morning, the rascal stevedore was taunting her about the scarlet ibis. The next moment, food-vendors – women supporting lovers or parasitic husbands – were shrieking with petrified patrons. Newsprint damp with blood shrouded the collapsed form. The woman was promptly dismissed from the Breakfast Shed. Six months later in court only Mister Harris was there for her; he signed the bond for the pregnant Lady Emelda.

'This ungrateful boy, beating that blasted pan just to drive out Mister Harris from the shack – where is he?' she asked of the two corbeaux fluttering down. 'Ah, Pockot deafening you birds too.'

Mister Harris coughed.

The two carrion-birds darted off from the tree outside her kitchen window. The wind with stench had winnowed the skeletal branches of most of its leaves. At the roots garbage mounted about the trunk shorn of its bark. Fierce pariah dogs combated among themselves for skeletons of fish sucked dry or bones already scraped of their meat.

Lady Emelda regretting her son's birth: 'I should of toss the child in the dump. Just another roasted stray-dog they would think the next morning. Or shove the bastard in a floursack and throw it in the Dry River on a rainy day.'

Seeing Pockot emerging from the blacksage bushes, she sighed, 'My cross, my cross . . .'.

Pockot marched in with the pan on his head.

'Always be grateful to you boss. Nobody decent does hire anybody from this slum. But you mammy promise the Potogee you giving up that pan and planning to take up some decent instrument like a guitar or something . . .'.

Lady Emelda thought she heard coughing from the bedroom.

Loudly she reminded – 'You hear last night with you own two ears how me and Mister Harris quarrelling the same bitter quarrel about that pan.'

It was always Mister Harris's conviction that the pan was like an African drum, transmitting sounds for violence. He was quick to mention how ready panmen during Carnival celebration crashed those oildrums on rival bands. The bevelled edges were like meat cleavers which with knives, ice-picks, and painted cutlasses, panmen gashed, stabbed and hacked away at their rival steelbands. It was a worse experience for doctors – sewing up stomachs, stitching arms, legs and faces. For the police, steelband violence was worse than revolutions.

'But that pan still keeping Pockot out of mischief,' was all Lady Emelda meekly argued.

Pockot was not clipping clothes-lines or filching undergarments left overnight soaking in oildrums of soapy water. He did not rustle up scrub-boards or furniture neglected just for a moment in broad daylight. He was not looting, like other young men around, throwing rocks at the train, or stripping cars of parts. He was not rustled up like the others for the recent robbery of a cloth-pedlar in Corbeaux City. Didn't even Mister Harris himself testify that at the time of the robbery Pockot was playing 'Jerusalem, the Golden' outside the shack?

While she combed his hair, Lady Emelda warned, 'You don't get rid of that pan, Mister Harris threat'ning to leave.' She sniffed his kerchief.

'Who give you that sweet perfume? Oh, Lawd, I hope you not mixed-up with some loose woman already.'

She rasped at his chin with a rough hand. 'You face smooth like bottle. You not man yet, boy.'

The cathedral bell, and briskly she shoved him through the doorway, watching him trotting down the dirt-lane, empty except for pariah dogs. Shortly Pockot was spanking the paved sidewalk of the city. A donkey-cart with coconuts had sunk into the molten asphalt.

A whip checked Pockot.

'You want to help, slum-thief, you thiefing bitch! I just see you come out from that slum. You think I forget how you panmen picked me clean of all my cloth like corbeaux.'

Pockot escaped amid the jeering from pedlars, congesting the sidewalks. He fled down a quiet street lined with wooden warehouses exuding the smell of crushed coffee. He entered a small square with an effigy of Christopher Columbus. A richer sort of beggars promptly reached out empty hats. One was with text: 'He that giveth to the poor, lendeth to the Lord.'

Pockot turned out his pocket. But he would return with his pan and play for them 'Jerusalem, the Golden'.

Their scorn drove him off. Confused, he avoided noisy, congested streets, and soon was striding briskly through Woodford Square. Hordes of preachers and political prophets shouted for his attention. Loiterers, occupying the octagonal bandstand where steelband competitions were held annually, seemed to jeer at him. Ragged mendicants unshaven for months regarded the boy with sudden hostility. They dug their arms into tarred bins for bits of food or ransacked piles of leaves fallen from the large flowering trees, shading the square.

A preacher, yet without text, pointed his staff at Pockot. He threatened fire and brimstone if his daily ration was not met. But the boy, hearing the cathedral bell, bolted for the grocery. Just then the half-crazed preacher found a text: 'The wicked flee when no man pursueth.'

Ten minutes late, Pockot was pleading with the Portuguese proprietor.

'Praying in church, eh?' he repeated. 'Well, the radio just announce some rogue was in the cathedral and emptied the box for the widow's mite.' He shook the ash from a fat cigar. 'Before my customers see two pan sticks in your pocket or before you empty my cash register – here's your pay and get your backside out of my premise – quick sharp,' shoving a small brown envelope into the boy's hand. 'Tell your mother, boy, I owe her nothing more.'

Directly Pockot headed for the Dry River, a concrete waterway winding through the city and emptying itself in the sea not far from the city dump. Sometimes there were rich finds of coins, cutlery, combs, or bright buttons along the river bed. Eddo bushes sprouted in the wavy silt where a crab or two could be found. But the brief fruitless search ended with rain clouds breaking malevolently above him. The slightest rainfall brimmed this river. Pockot imagined the slum-dwellers already fishing out bits of furniture, derelict motor-parts, and parts of houses long fallen into deep disrepair that the river had ripped away from the poorer part of the city.

Frantically he was dashing from tree to tree in the dismal downpour. His canvas shoes squelched and he thought about his new pair next to his ping pong pan under the canvas cot in his room.

'Not even a sheet of newspaper over you head, boy? Come shelter,' invited the deformed vendor, lifting a gunny sack of her makeshift shed. 'You want to ketch pleurisy or what?'

The cathedral bell gonged. The woman made a sign of the cross, reaching for her rosary, garlanding an upright with a cardboard placard. The charcoal letterings – oranges 1 per five, 2 for nine – challenged the boy's scant arithmetic.

The vendor, spotting the two sticks through the wet clothing, shuddering and stealthily crept a hand for her knife.

But Pockot wanted two oranges. Skilfully the woman dislodged two peeled oranges, one from either end of the base of the pyramid.

'Salt?' she queried, without enthusiasm, stating curtly, 'They is fresh oranges too. I peel them first thing this morning. I don't sell stale things like other people.' She flourished the knife.

Pockot deposited ten cents in her wet palm. She kept her eyes on him while she lifted a penny with her toes from an enamel plate under her bench.

The quote 'He that giveth to the poor . . .' was cut short.

The knife was flashed. 'Police! Police!'

Pockot, scampering away, saw the penny rolling ahead of him and slotting into a crack in the pavement.

'You fresh, forward bastard – trying to buy me with a penny. That sweet smell don't fool me. I old enough to be you mother. Beside I have a man, don't mind I does feed and clothe him.' The vendor was shouting as if there were an audience, 'You panmen wouldn't just let a poor widow earn a mite in a decent way, eh?'

Pockot might have flung himself into the swirling river. But many melodies were swirling in his brain, which he must play along with 'Jerusalem, the Golden' for those beggars. Those melodies would be the choice of calypsonians, too, and, during the carnival celebration, steelbands marching throughout the island would beat out his composition as the most popular road-tune for dancing crowds, tourists and natives alike.

The dark sky had made the day seem almost evening to him. Hungry, Pockot paused before a hooded stall. A pale, dyspeptic man in a black raincoat promised instant virility with his oysters and homemade peppersauce. He enticed the shivering boy with a sample, while an aged woman, reeking with perfume, winked enticingly at him. The vendor, splitting an oyster and squirting yellowish sauce from a green bottle, urged, 'Try this free one, boy, and if the old, fresh-up bitch don't bawl out, I pay you.'

The prostitute pushed Pockot off the sidewalk. 'The boy ain't have no hair yet.' A taxi beamed into view, the headlights revealing thin strokes of rain. The horn resonated through his head. 'You see a coffin you like, boy!' Amid the jeering Pockot galloped for home.

Lady Emelda had just bolted her kitchen window. 'Boy, I was just wondering who so damn foolish to be running through this wet rain. You want a good pneumonia to put you in the grave. I can't even afford a candle, much less a coffin.'

The boy's sudden entrance had forced Mister Harris to scurry back into his bedroom. Pockot dropped the pay-packet on the kitchen table. The mother promptly busied herself counting the earnings by the drooping flames of a kerosene lamp. Her regret was not being able to buy the length of polka-dot cloth from the pedlar robbed and beaten one bright day in Corbeaux City. But it was high time she shed her floursack dresses. About to ask her son if he had ever spotted that cloth-pedlar, Mister Harris coughed aloud.

'Ay, ay, boy, is it me who late cooking or what?' realising Pockot had come back much too early. But caught up in her counting, she thought, 'Maybe the boss give the boy time off to bring home the pay for his mammy.' Then, she put before him a hot cup of bush tea, her antidote for pneunomia or pleurisy, reciting, 'I remember the Potogee boss, boy. He had one big appetite. And so every day I uses to give him double servings of peas and rice and full up his glass with cold drinks, sorrel and sea-moss. Kind deeds does pay. Look today how he gone and give you a good job.'

Pockot shoved aside the bitter bush tea.

Twice then Mister Harris coughed.

Smoked coiled about the roof, leaking heavily now so that Lady Emelda hurriedly had to arrange pots and pans about the warped flooring. The wind drove water through gaping cracks in the plywood partitions. Pockot saw vermin crawling out from under the scruffed linoleum.

'What wrong you do, boy?' she exploded. 'Whole day my eyes blinking. Last night that bad dream about floods . . .'. She brought the pay envelope even closer. 'I hope my eyesight good enough – but a whole ten cents missing.'

The boy merely glared towards the bedroom.

'Boy, you didn't empty the Potogee man cash-register? Answer me.'

She splashed the tea across the table. She stamped and kicked over the water receptacles already brimming over. 'So bam!' she snapped her fingers. 'Just like that you lose the job . . .'.

Mutely, he avoided her glare.

'You ever does know what you mammy do to get you that job? I beg and beseech on these knees. Nobody want a slum boy to touch their grocery. They don't want to carry home lice and jigger in their groceries. These city folks think rat and cockroach follow people like Pied Pipers from this slum behind God's back. And after I give my honest word you not a pan-beating bastard like the others, the Potogee boss still remembered after all these years the kindness of this same Lady Emelda. . . . Ah, Pockot, you was my cross from the day you born.'

She dashed into his room. On re-entering the kitchen, she almost cracked his rib with the pan.

'This pan is the cause of all troubles. Your trouble, my trouble, and Mister Harris trouble. This pan is your original sin.'

Pockot hid his face but his ears seemed to have felt pain each time the crooked crowbar punctured the pan. Her aim was haphazard, but in the next few minutes Lady Emelda had gouged almost all thirty-two notes of the Ping Pong pan.

'It done,' she cried, clanging the bar upon the disfigured pan. 'Mark my word, boy, you going to end up in that same dump where you pick up this stray pan.'

No coughing came from the bedroom.

Turning to Pockot, she ordered – 'Go.'

He sensed her helplessness when she whispered, 'Mister Harris don't want you to eat he food no more . . .'.

Even faster than from the grocery Pockot fled from the shack. He was running through the rain as though chased by many demons.

'Go join those panmen and end up in jail,' she hoarsely shouted.

Steelband men in Corbeaux City ferociously protected their tent, housing their tuned oil-drums. But in the darkling afternoon the boy had crawled undetected into the tarpaulin tent and lay gasping on the wooden platform.

The tent was warmer than the shack. Pockot must have fallen asleep, for shortly he was awakened by the sound of a siren. Some stray cinder from the city dump finally must have set ablaze those shapeless shacks of Corbeaux City. But then he felt something cold against him, some flea-ridden bitch also seeking warmth.

All around the faces of pans gleamed as though to be recognised by him.

Pockot knew each by name: bass, cello, guitar, and tenor or ping-pong pan. The bass, created from a full-size oildrum with bottom removed, boomed three or four full notes. These blended with the five or six notes of the cello fashioned from a smaller oildrum, and played in pairs as a rule. Smaller than the cello but larger than the tenor, the guitar pan – also played in pairs – produced as many as fourteen distinct notes.

But none except the tenor pan with its thirty-two notes existed for Pockot at that moment. He himself was its creator. He removed it from its metal stand, adjusted its canvas strap around his spindly neck, and felt the bevel cool against his aching stomach. With his pair of rubber-tipped sticks he plied its surface, teasing out note after note.

After a while he was beating louder and louder as though to muffle the memory of his own pan. In the dimness of his tears he saw the grocery battered into pulps. The next moment the littered lane became clearer and from the darkened doorway of his shack he saw Lady Emelda hovering over the form of Mister Harris, shrouded with newsprint. His mother was brandishing a bloody knife, and calling for him. . . .

Just then, Pockot felt something at his feet. But there was no malevolence in the snap of the flea-ridden bitch who, roused by the pan, weakly shook itself, and limped out of the tent.

Alone, Pockot Wilberforce wept aloud. Perhaps for the first time he was hearing his own voice which a man first of all must recognise if indeed he is to be free. Playing 'Jerusalem, the Golden', the boy, as though liberated at last, wept even louder as he unwound his triumph on the pan.

The Dark Side of Being Nine

JONATHAN SMALL

Branwell was only six years old when he first saw Olivese the obeah woman. He didn't know why people were always whispering in fear of her, or why they called her an obeah woman, but he wasn't one bit afraid of her. From the first time he saw her on her bicycle, sitting on a saddle so high that she seemed like a giant, he had waved to her, and Olivese had waved back, giving the bell on her handlebar three brisk musical rings. She did that every time she passed the house. It came to mean something very special to Branwell. When the moon was full and she floated past the house ringing her bell, he would stand by the window wondering why the children on the street were running and screaming in fright. He told his mother he liked Olivese, and she jokingly told him that Olivese was going to turn him into a wood dove and make him coo all night if he wasn't careful.

One day Olivese stopped on her way home and began to talk with Branwell's mother. Branwell couldn't take his eyes off Olivese, and after an hour of talking and laughing his mother had said, 'Wait, you turn this boy stupid or what, Miss Olive? You got him doting on you like he's a puppy-dog. You bessa take him home with you, hear!'

After that day Branwell ran down the road to the very bottom near a gully where Olivese lived. His mother had moved into the village only a few months before and she was very strict about where he went, but she didn't mind him visiting Olivese. Around the house were a lot of nettle bushes which Olivese used for tea. Branwell steered clear of them after realising that they could sting, finding great comfort climbing the large flamboyant tree that straddled the yard like a ship. He would spend whole Saturday mornings clambering up and down the tree while his mother was in town shopping.

Branwell liked Olivese a bit too much. Although her face was dried up and shrivelled like an old black-eye pea, she knew how to make him laugh, and if she didn't see a smile on his face she tickled his ribs and threatened to report his mother to the Ministry of Health for letting him look like a cricket. The time he told her that his mother had gone selling Instant Money tickets in a place called Nelson Street, Olivese burst into a big laugh.

'Well, the Lord help you if she get back before midnight,' she exclaimed. 'You better come down at me this afternoon and eat something proper. Your mother is a joke and a half! She look like a refugee on the wrong side of the tracks herself. Ho ho, it better be tickets she trying with on Nelson Street! You come to Aunt Vee, soul. I going have to take you under my wing.'

That was three years ago. Now Branwell was nine, and nearly looked it. Olivese Baxton was still working obeah and the flamboyant tree was as beautiful as ever. Olivese was no longer prospering like a clam in bacterial waters, and Branwell hadn't grown thick and strong even though Olivese had shared with him countless pots of chicken stewed up in a provocative jambalaya. This upset Olivese. It didn't seem right that after her efforts to fatten him she could still pick out each rib in his body with her eyes closed. She had grown so fond of him now that it wrenched the strings of her heart to look at him straining on a bough in the flamboyant tree, legs dangling in mid-air as he prepared to do an acrobatic stunt. It was partly this exhibition of bones shooting through threadbare khaki that prompted her to borrow a sewing machine and credit yards of cloth from the peripatetic Indian salesman whom she disliked on principle and on sight.

'Trust me with a few yards of this and a few yards of that,' she told him, hiding her contempt under a show of humility since it was generally known that as quiet as the Indian looked, he was a ruthless warlock when it came to getting money for merchandise offered on credit. Olivese knew the power of a bit of psychology and was not going to forfeit the favour by appearing stiff-necked and proud while pleading penury and need.

'I got a little godson that does run about here naked as he born,' she said, larding her concern with a sympathetic groan, 'and I would really like to put some cold cash in your hands, but a man bounced me in town today and take off with my purse.'

Whatever thoughts might have flown through the Indian's mind, he said nothing. He gave her an innocuous gaze, neither smiled nor frowned, and reached into the large suitcase for the cloth with dragons that she had pointed out to him first.

'You really like this?' he asked, drawing out the print with fingers that seemed too feminine for anything but what it was doing.

Olivese questioned the dragons with a corrugated brow. She liked the pattern for herself. Her eyes disappeared behind speculative folds. The Indian watched her succinctly, accommodating himself to the odours of the house with a blandness that belied horror and disgust. For a moment altruism took a back seat in Olivese's mind as she pictured herself dolled up in a fancy maxi evening dress, dragons or no dragons. She nodded to temptation and said, 'Gimme a few yards of it. What a yard it is?'

The Indian held on to her words as if they were the wise words of instruction and made dapper movements with his feet, measuring the cloth.

'Eleven ninety-nine. Cheap, no?'

Olivese did not answer. Her eyes were pulling out other pieces of cloth – silks, rayon, cotton, gaberdine. She had been practising obeah for so many years and giving away so much counterfeit advice and so many powerless charms, that the truant brainchild that took her mind off Branwell did not wrinkle the ceremonial mask she wore when a deal was working in her favour. The news that she was leaving the village for good was still her own secret as far as she knew. Ever since her daughter had told her what to do to get a visa from the British High Commission Office in the island, she had taken a vow of secrecy. She had gone for a new passport, made several trips to a real-estate agency downtown, and had begun to shop for her going-away gear. She hadn't let any hints out of her mouth, not even when good-minded people made a point of asking after her grandchildren in London. Her daughter had three boys under ten and wanted Olivese to nursemaid them during her shifts at a large general hospital. Olivese had not told her outright that she was a fool if she thought she was giving up her sanity for the price of an air-ticket. And she didn't say anything about welcoming the chance to escape a financial drought. What she said was more in the manner of a diplomatic bull that revealed just enough of her mind to stop her daughter from imagining she was being used. Olivese knew there were great possibilities for an obeah practice wherever there was a community of superstitious West Indians, and all she could think of was her name in blinking red letters that read: *Madame Olive, Spiritual Healer and Adviser.*

Olivese looked past the Indian's muddy blankness at herself getting on board the British Airways plane with yards of free sea-island cotton gracing her body. She concentrated on the business in hand with a bit of the Indian's sphinx.

'I think I'll have a few yards of this and five yards of that,' she said decidedly, taking the liberty to delve into the suitcase for the peach-coloured silk material and another with delicate flowery designs.

'This not for a boy,' the Indian said flatly, pursing his lips.

'I know, could dear! I taking this for me. I want the brown gaberdine for Branny. How much the silk?'

'This one is twenty dolla a yard, and that is fourteen-ninety-nine.'

Olivese noticed the austere glint in his eyes. She felt like returning him a full gaze that carried her foul opinion of him, but she mentally ticked him off as a suspicious old fool, saying, 'I can pay for it. Put it down in the book, man. My godson going look real nice in this piece of cloth. It just like his skin.'

She didn't dare look into the suitcase again for fear of goading the Indian into serious mental reservations, but as if to assure her that she had nothing to fear he gave her a little smile and said, 'This is five yards of gaberdine. If you take all I give you a discount.'

'How much a discount that?'

'Ten per cent.'

Olivese demurred, then nodded brightly. 'Go 'head. It could make him four pants. I'll pay you next week when you come around. You does have to make hay while the sun shine. You coming next Friday as usual?'

The Indian unbuttoned his lips, pausing in the act of tying up his suitcase. 'You will see me next Friday at half past five.'

Olivese savoured the moment of success with a straight, dull face. 'God willing, I'll see you next week Friday evening.'

It was a while before she packed the materials away in a box that sat next to the sewing machine in her bedroom. Many years had gone by since she had worked as a shirt stitcher and pants cutter in a local garment factory. Nevertheless she knew her skills, and it would only be a matter of days before things were cut out and pinned together in recognisable patterns. The thought that she was burdening herself unnecessarily towards the end fizzed out of her mind as she thought of Branwell decked out in his new pants, reminding his mother how she had godmothered him. That alone justified taking an underhand swipe at the Indian, and the evening grew heavy with insect-sound and the frequent drip of self-congratulation that was without alarm or discomfort.

That night at half-past seven there was a knock on Olivese's door. It was Branwell. He had recently begun insisting on watching the television news with her, and if his mother was out on a spree, he stayed on until she collected him. He stood on the doorstep like a stray animal, eyes pulping and red from tears.

'Fancy you crying, man, shame!' Olivese said hugging him tightly. Branwell hugged her back barely able to get his arms around her waist. 'What wrong with you now, cry-baby man?'

'Ma say you going to England and ain' coming back,' Branwell sobbed.

Olivese marshalled her feelings and pushed him gently away so that she could look down straight into his face. The wrinkles in her own face ran in all directions as she laughed and said, 'Somebody making sport. Who tell she so?'

Branwell stared mutely, pouting.

'I tell you already your mother head bad, Bran-boy! I may be going away, but not to any cold dirty England.' She pulled him cheerfully into her skirt again, rubbing his coarse overgrown hair. 'You crying because I taking a little vacation? What kinda man you? You make me shame! Come lemme show you what I bought for you, do!'

He followed her dutifully into the next room, rubbing his eyes. There was no expectant glimmer on his face when Olivese bent over the box where she had placed the material and brought out the folded gaberdine. His face was dead. Olivese cringed mentally, but pulled a face that was guaranteed to make him smile. He stared at her stolidly.

'It is yours,' she said at last, seeing the situation for what it was. 'I going make you some pants before I go away. You like it?'

Branwell nodded without jubilation.

'You sure?'

'Yes, I like it, Aunt Vee,' he answered this time.

'Well, next thing we have to do is measure you for it. You like this for a shirt?' she asked, caressing the sea-island cotton.

Branwell gave the cloth a lacklustre stare and circumvented the question. 'How many shirts you making, Aunt Vee?'

'I going make you three, so that you won't have to say you don't have nothing to wear to Sunday School. Your mother tell me she sending you to the Pilgrim Holiness. She should be thinking 'bout sending herself. You don't mind her. You go 'long and study the Bible hard, and pray for your Aunt Vee. But where your mother is tonight?'

The little face began to set up again, ready to tremble with tears. He held them back with a sniffle and said, 'My Dad came for Ma. They gone out in the car.'

'Where she going now in that breaking-down car?'

'I don't know.'

'She tell you when she coming back?'

'She tell me stay here till she get back.'

Olivese sucked her teeth, real vexed with Branwell's mother. 'She really want locking up. If I could take you with me I would, so you have somebody to treat you like a human. Your mum ain't fit to raise nettles. She out night and day and poor you don't know where she gone half the time. Supposing you took ill or something?'

Branwell didn't have the answer to that. He was already feeling ill. After his parents had driven away he had rolled around in his mother's bed bawling his lungs out and banging his head on the metal headrest by accident. The bang had given him a headache.

Olivese closed her eyes, but she wasn't praying. 'She feed you anything today – apart from bread and sweet drink?'

Branwell snorted and swallowed hard. 'Ma ain' cook. I had tea and Pa started talking to me.'

Olivese kept her anger intact, frowning as if the devil was riding her face. 'Look, come out here and eat some of this rice and stew and tell me what he was saying that take him so long to say,' she said, heading towards the kitchen. 'My friend in Carrington Village bring me some beef and I put it together with some vegetables I had knocking around. What your father was saying, the no-good?'

'He tell me I have to live with him in Silver Sands.'

Olivese gave a good laugh and slapped her hands together. She knew Branwell's father by sight. He was a fisherman who spent more time in the city than at sea, and he was always borrowing money. When he wasn't pestering Branwell's mother, he was troubling other women. Even before knowing him as Branwell's father Olivese had said shooting was the only way to get rid of him.

'I suppose he going feed you on crab milk and sprats,' she laughed cynically. 'Look, you better off with your mother, never mind she down Nelson Street selling tickets half the time. At least she knows how to make cornmeal pap and fishcakes. You stay right here on Willoughby Road where Miss Johnson and Peggy can keep an eye on you when I gone. I won't be gone that long, and when I come back I want to see you right here wearing my shirts and pants, you hear?'

She shook an admonitory finger at Branwell before turning to place a frying pan on a grease-stained gas stove. Branwell didn't follow her movements. He sat on a chair with broken cane, thinking. His mother had told him that Peggy Johnson had told Mrs Johnson that she had heard that Olivese had applied for an entry certificate into England, and she had seen Olivese herself going into the building where the British High Commission had its offices. Peggy was Mrs Johnson's daughter who worked in the city as somebody's secretary. Branwell's mother didn't know where Peggy worked. Peggy had told her that she could sit in her office and see clear across the city, and Branwell's mother had said she must be working in a high-up job.

Everybody on Willoughby Road had a great respect for Peggy, and when she spilled the news about Olivese's plans to travel, embroidering it with the further news that Olivese had put the house up for sale together with its contents, those who heard had every reason to believe her. One thing with the Johnsons was that they knew everybody's business, but nobody knew theirs, and they were selective about whom they shared news with. Not always wisely selective, for Peggy had told Branwell's mother about Olivese, wanting something to talk about travelling in a mini-bus into the city, and Branwell's mother was not born with a lid on her mouth. Another thing about the Johnsons was that they were not afraid of Olivese. They ridiculed her obeah powers, Mrs Johnson using her jalousies as spy holes and laughing her head off at the fools emerging from Olivese's house filled with mumbo-jumbo. Mrs Johnson and Peggy were seldom wrong, so Branwell had hung on to his mother's words, sick with the fear that Olivese was about to abandon him.

Olivese stirred the pan, setting up her face like a black cloud. She couldn't do a thing about deceiving the child, and it was useless to let her wrath burst on his head, since he was only repeating his mother. The guilt she felt about betraying him was assuaged by the confidence that the milk of her heart had not been wasted. She had given him a sense of security and love when his mother went off seeking her jollies on Nelson Street and elsewhere. The fact that gossip had got into the village to hasten the trauma of separation broke her own heart. It wasn't as if she wasn't going to tell him she was going away. She was going to tell him at a time she deemed right in her wisdom, and he would know that it was permanent in the first letter she wrote from England.

Her heart felt as heavy as an axe-head as she stirred the stew, wondering who gave Peggy Johnson the right to disturb the emotional balance she was able to accomplish in a child who had become dog-meat between an irresponsible mother and father. It was her natural ability to charm and amuse people that had drawn Branwell out of the miserable muteness of a hurt life. All that she had achieved in three years was about to go up in smoke.

Turning to Branwell she gave a prefatory chuckle and said, 'You know the coolie man that does come around on a Friday evening? It is he that sold me the cloth. I buy this house thirty years ago and he's the first Indian that ever set foot inside it. I don't have uses for Indians, too slick – and they just like to use black people to get rich. If you see him coming down here before Friday, run and let me know. I going know how to deal with him.'

Olivese got no reply from Branwell, and she didn't press for one. She scooped the stew into an enamel plate and began to hum a mission song that suddenly found its way into her head. Branwell bent over in his chair, watching the floor through a fresh film of tears. Olivese placed the plate on a small kitchen table covered with red chequered linoleum.

'I know you want to watch television, but come, soul. You can watch TV after you fill up that hole your windbag mother leave for gas to settle in. What she say when your father start talking crazy?'

Branwell broke into a convulsive sob. 'She said he was free to take me to Alaska. She doesn't like me, Auntie Vee – and I hate my dad!'

'Poor you, she ready to hand you over like some Herod, but not while I have something to say,' Olivese said, standing over him. 'Your mum loves you but she doesn't have one grain of sense in her head and no backbone. If I wasn't 'fraid of prison I'd drop a few lashes in her backside and set her thinking straight.' She reached for his hands. They were pressed tightly against his face. 'Don't worry, she can't give you away to that no-good. There ain't much to choose between the two of them, but the law won't let him touch you. You have rights.'

Branwell allowed her to kiss him and wipe his eyes with the hem of her skirt. It had a sweet camphor smell, but he didn't enjoy it. He limped over to the table and sat down before the steaming plate, ready to erupt in bitterness again.

Olivese combed her fingers through his hair affectionately and said, 'You might as well eat up. I was going to get you some ice cream today. Your Aunt Vee getting old and forgetful. Miss Hackett shop don't shut early Friday nights. I going step down the road and get you some now, some nice creamy cherry-vanilla. When you eat the ice-cream I going measure you up for the clothes.'

Branwell began to cry into the food in earnest. Olivese turned away, hiding grief that blew out her face into clownish puffs. She knew what was happening to the boy, and she felt powerless to undo the damage. When she reached the semi-dark bedroom and found her purse still safely sandwiched between the pillows on her bed she heard him bawling: 'Why you selling the house if you coming back soon?'

Olivese steadied herself and burst into a bitter laugh. 'Ho, ho, so now I selling the roof over my head! The people in this village don't have nothing to do but watch one another and speculate. You can't take them seriously, or you could do them a' evil. The TV didn't turn on yet because I was down in the back washing my hair, and this old rope is trouble. I going turn it on now, and you can watch the movie after the food. And stop crying, everything going be all right!'

Olivese kept the television set in the front-house – the term for the drawing-room of two-gabled wooden houses. It was a tidy room, with old pock-marked mahogany furniture that still had a shine. She turned on the set and waited for it to light up.

Without going back into the other room to look at Branwell she said, 'All right, Brannie, it on, but don't you get up before you put some food in your stomach. I feel like a little walk in truth, but I won't be gone long. Relax yourself till I come back.'

Branwell heard the front door locking him in with a noisy *click* and threw the fork out of his hand. The lie Olivese had told him had taken away all his feeling for food. All he wanted to do was make her sorry for turning against him like everybody else. Somewhere in the spiralling mist that his mind had become, two deaths formed a single image of unhappiness that told him what he should do. He had seen one death only a few weeks before. It was that of a woman in a television story. The woman had drunk poison because she was suffering from a bad disease and her husband had left her. The other death had happened a long time ago, when his mother and father were living together at Silver Sands. They had given him a dog – the most beautiful long-eared dog he had ever seen – and it became a family idol that couldn't do any wrong until the day nine steaks of fried dolphin disappeared from the kitchen table. The fish was the end of the dog's story. Branwell's father poured kerosene down his throat and left him for two days behind the yard paling where he rolled up and died. The sight of his golden-haired dog covered with flies was grotesque, and it was Branwell who helped his mother bury it in the soft sandy soil at the back of the house.

Branwell knew Olivese kept a can of kerosene oil in the kitchen under the sink unit. The kerosene was a standby. Olivese used it for cooking if she ran out of bottled gas, or if a power cut forced her to use her old oil lamp. Sometimes she used it to kill ants and centipedes in the garden.

Branwell found the can of oil behind a large box of detergent. He unscrewed the lid, dizzy with the thought of his own death. His life meant nothing to anyone. No one would miss him. At first oil gushed out over his cheeks, then he fixed the hole securely to his mouth. He gulped the oil down as if it was a cold frothy glass of mauby. For a moment there was no real sensation of pain. Then it hit him, rising from the pit of his stomach. It felt like the unleashing of a dozen sharp-edged pocket knives cutting right through the centre of his body. He fell to the floor, wondering if his mother would miss him. It didn't matter any more who missed him. All he wanted to do was find another life.

PART III

'This is What She Had Been Missing Without Really Knowing'

Home and Exile

Exile

ANTHONY LOCKHART

For me London is an ordered and predictable existence. This morning when I rise, Yvonne has already left for the West End so I have a bath, dress and make myself a cup of coffee which I have while I go over the notes for my day's lectures. My students at the Poly demand little of me: just an elucidation of basic principles and an outline of the most fashionable theories. For extras I throw in personal anecdotes to illustrate the point that one should never underestimate personalities or social factors in public administration. After I have reviewed my notes I walk down the hill to the train, and my day in public life begins.

The train is delayed, and to pass the time I buy a copy of *The Times*. I write a column for a West Indian paper which is on the newsstand at the station, but since I get a copy at work I disregard it and page through *The Times*. On page four is an item from home. The Prime Minister has had a heart attack and the Minister of Trade, Industry, Tourism and Development is acting as Prime Minister by consensus of the Cabinet. So my man has made it, I say to myself, as the train comes snaking around a corner, and I step forward on the platform.

After my lectures I go to the library to write my columns. On the train I had decided to analyze the Prime Minister's achievements, but in the library, with the heater on and my skin prickling, I cannot find the words. Something within says, wait, there might be more to this than a heart attack so I go back to my office, call my editor, Jonathan Blake, and tell him I will submit an in-depth piece when the Prime Minister's condition has stabilized.

'But suppose he dies?' Jonathan asks.

'Then I may write no more columns for you,' I say, surprising myself with the admission that I would contemplate returning.

At Charing Cross I buy an evening paper and as I wait for advice on my train to be posted on the board, I skim through the paper for an update from home. There is nothing. Perhaps no news is good news, I say to myself, and get a Mars bar.

'I heard today your Leader's ticker almost stopped,' Yvonne casually says as I come through the front door and enter the living room where she is looking at television.

'How do you know that?' I ask.

'One of the prop men at the theater. Said one of his relatives from your island phoned him during the night. Apparently the "Beeb" had a news crew in the region so they flew across.'

I go to the kitchen for a beer. When I return I offer Yvonne a sip, but she waves me away. I throw myself into a chair, pick up a book I had left on the floor last night and try to read. It is no use. Memories from home keep forcing themselves on me, probing, teasing, challenging me to go back over the incidents that had prompted my departure.

Suddenly I hear Yvonne say, 'Look, Desmond. Here it comes.'

I look up from my reveries in the past, and magically I am transported back to the island I had left a year and a half ago. John, my best friend, is there, so is Margaret, my wife; and my Minister too, the man who had so much confidence in me but who could not support me in my crisis. I am back at home, yet something is wrong. Margaret is saying that the Prime Minister is in a stable condition while John is promising a full statement in the morning from my Minister who seems too benumbed to speak.

'Oh, hell, I can't believe this,' I say. 'The man is dead, and they are still afraid he'll get up and cuss the whole lot of them for abrogating his authority.'

'What on earth are you talking about?' Yvonne asks. 'Your wife, the elegant British-trained personal physician of the PM, says his condition is stable.'

'My wife is a sycophantic fool,' I shout. 'Even after I resigned she went to the Prime Minister to ask him not to accept my letter. Now the man is dead, and she is afraid to tell the world so.'

'How do you know he is dead?'

'I just know.'

'Well, you can tell the "Beeb" so when they come calling,' Yvonne says. 'They did say they were trying to reach Dr Desmond Jones, former aide to the Acting Prime Minister for his comments.'

On the late-night news I am amused to see what the broadcasters have made of their attempted interview with me. Make no mistake about it: the British have learned much about the media from their American counterparts whose sensationalism is the daily fare back home. For a few minutes I am catapulted into notoriety. There are pictures of Oxford, my four bedroom mansion at home, the Polytechnic and my South-East London flat where I live with an actress from the 'more avant-garde section of the West End', and I cannot suppress the laughter when, in a very smug Oxford accent which, of course, I put on for the occasion, I appear on the screen with pipe in hand and say to their questions, 'I have no comment,' words which might have kept me my job at home had I used them more often.

I do not go to bed before I have finished my column. The Prime Minister's heart attack, I write, is the reward for his attempt to superintend and control every aspect of national life in an attempt to promote a distorted notion of what modern government is all about. Moreover, the reporting of the story of his heart attack by one of the world's most reputable media houses is yet another indication of the failure of the Western media to accurately cover events in the so-called Third World. The international image of the Prime Minister in no way squares with the systematic and sophisticated intimidation he practised domestically, and I finish the column by telling the tales of two colleagues who were among several hounded out of the land of their birth.

By the time the column is complete Yvonne is asleep. For me sleep is long in coming, and I go over the day's events and remember my escapades at home. My article is not the whole truth, I concede. Its portrayal of the Prime Minister might be accurate, but could he have achieved so much without the complicity of others? Look how many times I had urged John, who was trusted to reason with the Prime Minister, but he dared not incur his wrath. And what of my fellow mandarins, empty-headed and insecure, concerned with trips to workshops and conferences and with promoting their courtesans to positions close to them?

Early next morning I call Jonathan at his home.

'Look Jonathan, I can't give you a column,' I say, 'but I can give you a scoop. The Prime Minister died since yesterday. Ask your man down there to go to the Acting Prime Minister immediately and tell him I know already.'

'Does this mean that I don't get any more columns?' Jonathan asks.

'I suppose so,' I say and hang up.

I look up from the phone, and Yvonne is standing before me with a mug in each hand. In her duster she looks smaller than she actually is, and I feel a sudden need to protect her.

'It's coffee,' she says.

I take a mug and we sip coffee in the silence of unspoken words. I am bewildered at the strength of the ties with home. Life here has made no demands on me, and yet I would go back to the frustrating and back-biting narrowness of the island.

'Why did you tell Jonathan you couldn't give him a column?' Yvonne asks in the subdued voice that so often suggests hurt. 'I saw what you wrote, and it's good.'

'But it's not the whole story.'

'What is then – the four-bedroom house and your dear Margaret?'

'That's not fair,' I say.

'Isn't it?' Yvonne asks, looking straight at me. 'You aren't going to write any more columns for Jonathan, are you?'

'No, I am not.'

'Why? Are you thinking of going back now that your nemesis is dead and your protector has been elevated?'

'I don't know, Yvonne,' I say. 'I really don't know.'

Yvonne rises from the chair, and as she leaves the room I put my head in my hands. Half an hour later the front door closes, and the house is suddenly empty and cold.

The day goes badly. I have been too razzled by Yvonne's behaviour to go over my notes properly, and my lectures are not among my most inspired. Some of my students have seen me on television. They come to classes with expectations of behind-the-scenes revelations, and I take a certain perverse delight in seeing their eager faces give way to boredom as I say nothing about the events at home.

Today is one day that I'm glad for the traditional English reserve, for only one student, in whom I discern a Jamaican accent, dares to ask about the events at home, and I simply say that I do not wish to comment at the moment.

Jonathan's call in the early afternoon brightens the day somewhat. 'You were dead right, Desmond,' he says to me. 'Your man called me himself and asked me not to go with the story before he made his announcement. Something about laying the groundwork for an orderly transition of power.'

You bet, I say to myself as I imagine my Minister – why do I still call him mine? – manoeuvring to blunt the influence of the city clique.

'So you didn't get your scoop?' I say.

'Small matters. Your man offered me an exclusive interview and said he would fly me down for it. By the way, he sends you his greetings. Says he wishes he could do something for you, but his hands are tied.'

There is a short item on the news tonight. The weather has suddenly turned cold, and I watch it with a mug of cocoa and a sweater. Emmanuel Chambers, the man who brought thirteen years of stability to the previously stormy island of Clemencia, is dead at the age of sixty-eight. His successor, Jerome Burton, former Minister of Trade, Industry, Tourism and Development, in praising Mr Chambers' achievements, promises to continue his efforts at nation-building. This time neither John nor Margaret appears, and there are no references to a lecturer at a London polytechnic.

London returns to its predictability. The weather grows colder, darkness comes earlier and I begin to sense a void. Still, I am not worried, for at home the onset of the wet season would find me depressed and unfulfilled. The lectures which, in my earlier days at the Polytechnic, were labours of love, now become routine like rising and going to the office had become after seven years at home.

Talking to Yvonne does not help. Her intelligence is intuitive and visceral, and my lengthy attempts at mood analysis often send her to sleep. Besides, her play has begun. It is running longer than anticipated, and she is peeved that I have not come to see it.

'Your trouble,' she says to me one night, 'is that you refuse to open yourself up to your own spontaneity. I know how you feel but the play might be an eye opener for you.'

She is right. At home Margaret had been on the Cultural Council whose functions I avoided, and remembering the muddle our life had become, I relent. One chilly evening, when the train is late, I venture into the West End. With a certain trepidation that I might be out of place I enter the theatre, only to discover that people as respectable as I believe myself to be are waiting for the curtain. When it rises I am transported to a world of scenes I have long forgotten, and my life returns to me. At the final curtain, mumbling apologies to everyone

I go past, I find Yvonne backstage. She kisses me, changes quickly and we go home.

The next morning I wake early and roll out of bed without waking her. Feeling my way through the darkness I stumble down the stairs to the kitchen. The coffee's taste is sharp and evocative of mornings on the island. I put the cup on the table, go to the front room for paper and a pen and, sitting down, I return to the island, find a small boy of seven in a tenement yard in Newcastle and seek to capture every memory that his tears yield.

The week before Christmas the boy is in London. Here he will meet his wife at a dance to raise funds for an obscure island Party, heir to the void of the Newcastle mulatto to which his putative father had belonged.

'It's fascinating,' Yvonne says one evening as we sit on the rug in the front room, surrounded by walnut shells and pages and pages of my handwriting, 'but it's so unstructured. What you must do is ask Jonathan to recommend an editor.'

So the ordered life of London is disrupted. Now, once a week, I go North to a district of which I have always been wary to see Martin who promises to publish my 'novel'. Over the sherry which I have brought we sit in a corner of his bookshop whose showcase window the Front has already smashed, and this gentle, greying man with the voice of Job's patience, an exile too, teaches me the craft of fiction.

'But this is not fiction in the true sense of the word,' I protest one afternoon.

Martin smiles, a smile of indulgence perhaps.

'If it isn't,' he says, 'why all the concern with mood and atmosphere and the attempts to suggest a world beyond the word?'

'You tell me,' I ask, suddenly angry at his calm detachment, so reminiscent of the intransigence of colleagues who could not understand my impatience with the bureaucracy we had inherited from the British.

'Because you are an artist,' he says. 'Crude and untutored but an artist nonetheless. This work has power but it must be crafted if it is to be published.'

On my way back I leave the tube at Leicester Square and walk a little to ease the anger. There is a garbage strike, and the picture of garbage bags piled up on street corners with rats rummaging through them seems as incongruous with storybook images of London as the way in which the snow is slushy and black on the streets.

The light is on in the bedroom so I shout out, 'I'm home.' Even after the train ride flashing past sedate stations and monstrous apartments, I am still tense so I make myself a cup of chocolate and write for an hour.

When I enter the bedroom the light is off so I undress in the darkness, shivering in the moments between taking off my shirt and pulling on the woollen T-shirt in which I sleep.

'How did your session with Martin go?' Yvonne asks as I am about to get into bed.

'The usual,' I say and drape my hand across her shoulders.

'There is a letter on the table for you,' she says and I sense the restraint in her voice. 'From John . . . I imagine.'

The handwriting is John's but the envelope is official and there are no stamps.

'I think I will let it wait until the morning,' I say and turn off the light.

'No, Desmond, read it now,' Yvonne says and I know she is close to tears.

I turn the light back on and tear the edge of the envelope. Perhaps my tiredness deprives the moment of significance for I feel nothing as I extract the sheet of white paper. 'Dear Dr Jones, I have been directed by the Prime Minister to offer you . . .'. I read to the end and hand the letter to Yvonne. She turns on her back, dries her eyes on the quilted blanket and reads. Even the paper does not crackle as the snow falls lightly against the window.

When she folds the letter and gives it back to me the question is in her eyes. I get up, go to the dressing table and pull out my drawer. When I turn there is an envelope in my hand. I brandish it theatrically.

'The day after tomorrow we leave for Greece,' I say. 'These are the tickets. It is sunny there and I should be able to finish my book.'

Flying the Flag

JOHN GILMORE

The boy walked briskly up the long path, his well-polished black shoes crunching on the gravel. It was Saturday afternoon and Mr Knight had given him an exeat, but he had to be back at the school by six.

There was no one else in sight. He stopped to prod with his toe a conker which had fallen from one of the trees which lined the path. He took off his black kid gloves and tried to stuff them into the left-hand pocket of his grey tweed jacket but that was where he had put the book he had just bought in the local town – a paperback called *Wonders of the Universe* – so he put them in the right-hand pocket instead and then he picked up the conker.

He stood admiring it, still in its coat of green, the spikes of which were all bendy and soft, not like the hard spiky shell of the thing at home which was a bit like it. This was a horse-chestnut and the other was a horse-nicker, but why horse? His mother had complained when he had brought one into the drawing-room at home.

'Olly! take that nasty thing out of here! I don't care what it's called, and who told you that anyway? Lydia? Honestly, Gerald, that boy spends far too much time in the cook's company.'

One day at the other school Pollard had rubbed the hard, smooth, shining grey of a horse-nicker seed on the hard, dull, grey cement of the form-room steps and pressed it on to the bare flesh of Oliver's thigh just below the hem of the khaki uniform shorts so that he could see how hot it could get.

Oliver dropped the green bits on the gravel and rubbed the conker round and round between his palms before he pelted it as far as it would go into the neighbouring field. Mr Knight had told him that the fields on each side of the path were out of bounds. Mr Knight hadn't said anything about throwing conkers into them.

Oliver wiped his hands on his jacket and put his gloves on again. None of the other boys wore gloves – they asked him if he thought it was winter already – but his mother had been very particular about the gloves.

'A gentleman always wears gloves when he goes out, Olly.'

Why was it so important to wear gloves here? His father never wore gloves, and his father was a gentleman, and an important one on the island too; he was the Chief Engineer at the Water Works Department – 'Willie Wife Dead' was what Pollard had once tried to tell him the initials stood for – and he was a member of the Yacht Club. It was all something to do with being At Home. Oliver had been born on the island and before his mother had brought him over to leave him at the school he'd only been to England once, when his father had brought them over on Home Leave, but of course England was Home. A lot of people who'd never left the island called it that too, when they weren't calling it the Mother Country, but of course the island was home too.

'That's because wherever your father and I are is always your home, Olly.'

Oliver walked up the path, wondering what Pollard would be doing at that very moment. There weren't any black boys at this school. It was strange only having white people around. The whole school was strange. So many things were different from the way they were at the other school, although that was a good school. His parents always said it was the best school on the island. But this one must be better, for his mother had explained to him how important it was for him to get a good English education so that he would know where he came from.

He had been here three weeks, and there was still always something new and different to learn. It had started on that other Saturday afternoon right after his mother had left him in the entrance hall with Mr Knight and gone off to catch her plane. He knew he would have to share a dormitory, but it had turned out to be such a small room, and there were six beds in it. The bigger boy who had helped him take his trunk up had just left him there. A small label was stuck to the head end of each of the cream-painted iron bedsteads. Calvert,

Bain, Frognal, Robinson. . . . The other two were Meade and Ross. There was a cupboard beside each bed, with a curtain in front of it instead of a door, and all the curtains were worn and faded like the ones in Lydia's room in the servants' quarters at home. He unlocked the trunk and began to unpack.

Oliver opened the leather-covered photograph frame and put it at the front of the top shelf of the cupboard. There was a crisp, professionally-taken colour photograph in each section of the frame. His mother on one side, his father on the other. He looked in his wallet and took out a small, crumpled, black and white ping-pong photograph of a black woman in a starched white uniform cap. He put the photograph of Lydia into the leather-covered frame on the same side as his mother's picture. At first the top of it covered his mother's chin, but he jiggled it around under the glass until it didn't.

He went into the trunk again and, from the middle of a pile of shirts, took out a small, flat, round piece of wood and a small, brightly-coloured flag on a thin stick. He fitted the stick into the hole in the base and put the flag next to the photograph frame. He was glad Pollard had given him the flag on the last day of term at the other school. He hadn't seen Pollard during the vacation. He'd been too busy getting ready to come to England and anyway his mother didn't like him to ask friends over to the house. When he had had his birthday party in August it had been his mother who had invited all the other children.

The flag meant that the island was now Independent. That meant that they didn't have a Governor from England any more. There was a local man in Government House, a black man, and now he was called the Governor-General. 'At least the Queen is still the Queen, thank God!' his father had said.

And then Oliver was no longer alone.

'You the new boy then?'

'That's rather a cissy name, isn't it? We just use last names here.'

'What's that funny flag?'

'Don't take Calvert's bed whatever you do, or he'll bash your face in. He's a big bruiser.'

'How come you're not a wog?'

'What kind of a car's your Dad got? Mine's got a Jaguar. It goes ever so fast; it can do a ton up the motorway.'

'That your nanny in the picture? Look, Bain, Robinson's got a black nanny!'

'Ohh! The *cook* . . .'

'Must be frightfully rich to be having servants like that.'

'You any good at cricket?'

The bell for supper put an end to the questions.

Calvert had turned up on the Sunday. He was quite small and wore glasses. He asked Oliver if it was true that humming-birds could hover in one place.

On the Monday school had started. There were only fifty boys or so in the boarding-house, and from a quarter to nine they melted into the hundreds in the main school. During registration somebody sniggered when Oliver called the teacher 'Sir'. He got his timetable sorted out. He'd done French and Latin before, as well as Spanish, but they didn't do Spanish in this school, so they made him do German instead. 'You'll soon catch up,' the master had said, but even though Calvert helped him with the prep sometimes, it was hard. Everybody else his age had been here three or four years already, and their uniforms weren't new.

The first lesson the first day after Assembly was French. While they were waiting for the master, Oliver looked at the textbook. It wasn't the same series they used at the school back home. The other boys were noisy. When Oliver stood up because the master came in, they giggled. When he asked the master a question in French, somebody let out a long whistle.

'Hark at him. Il parley Frog!' It was Bain.

After the class, one of the day-boys pushed him up against a wall.

'You trying to show us all up, mate? You trying to be funny? Don't do it again, will you? or you just might happen to have a little accident, know what I mean?'

Oliver didn't speak French again except when the master told him to.

One afternoon in the main school lunch-room, after they'd all had baked beans for lunch, Meade had leaned his chair back and cocked up his legs while he held a burning cigarette lighter next to the seat of his pants. Then he let out a series of farts which turned into long blue flames.

Everything about the place smelt. The food was awful. The dorm smelt. The cleaners came round during the day when they were down at the main school, but most of the boys only took a bath once a week when the bath-roster said that they had to. And he knew now why after lights-out the first night he'd heard Ross call out to Meade 'Hey, Pus-face! Keep it quiet!' By the end of each week Meade's bed always smelt of stale spunk. The games changing-room smelt of the damp clothes in the big rows of wire lockers. He wished he didn't have to play rugby. It was always cold outside and it was like cricket at home. Why did everybody get so excited about running around after a ball? And you had to get changed in the big cold smelly room in front of everybody else. Sometimes a few of the black boys from the village went into the sea with no swimsuits on, but apart from that Oliver had never seen other people naked. In the school back home, people used to go into the toilet to take off the khaki shorts they wore for class and put on the navy ones they wore for games. Only the big boys wore long trousers for cricket. And after your games afternoon you went home to bathe.

It was just as bad having a bath in the boarding-house. There was no lock on the door and all the washbasins were in the same room and anybody could come in any time. The first time he'd had a bath in there he'd finished and was drying himself when Ross and Bain and Bain's big friend Plummer from Dorm 4 had come in and he'd wrapped the towel around his middle and they'd laughed at him.

'Little Olly doesn't want us to see what he's got! We'd better take a look at him, hadn't we?'

And Plummer had snatched off the towel and he'd tried to cover himself with his hands but Plummer grabbed his wrists.

'Is Mummy's boy shy then?' and held his hands up above his head while Bain got the heavy wet towel and moved about flicking it with swift stinging strokes at his balls and bum while they all three laughed at him.

'Stop it, please, stop it!'

'Ohh! please, please stop it,' they mocked. Plummer let him go. 'Give him his towel back, then,' Plummer said. 'Oh, right,' said Bain, and threw it into the bath-tub which was still full of dirty water. Then the three of them went off to the long row of basins on the other side of the big room to clean their teeth and left him alone.

But he didn't cry. It was very important not to cry. Boys who cried deserved all they got and would get more besides. It was almost as bad as sneaking. That was what it said in all the books about English schools which he'd read in the school library back on the island.

Plummer was in the year above. That was why he was in a different dorm. He was the captain of the under-fifteens and he was ever so strong. Plummer and Bain would say 'Let's play a tune on Robinson' and then they'd grab Oliver and twist his arm behind his back and give him a Chinese burn and grind their knuckles into his ribs or maybe they'd do it in a different order and sometimes they'd do other things as well and they all hurt but they hurt in different ways and they made Oliver make different kinds of noises while Plummer and Bain laughed at him. But he didn't cry. It was very important not to cry.

Oliver came round the last corner of the path. The big wrought-iron gates with their gilt salamanders were only twenty yards away and he would be in time for tea. The buns were delivered from an outside bakery and all the kitchen did was to put them out on a table in the boarding-house dining-room, still on the big metal tray on which they were delivered. They were much nicer than anything made in the boarding-house kitchen and Oliver could already imagine the thick currant-filled lumps of one of the buns filling up his stomach. But why did the tea have to have milk in it? The kitchen staff brought it out in a great big shiny urn, strong and with the milk in it already. They had English maids here. Back home his parents drank Earl Grey. It was much nicer. The tea here was nasty.

You weren't supposed to have more than one bun, but there were always some left over, and you could get two if one of the prefects didn't see you. If he could get two buns he wouldn't have to eat much supper. He could go upstairs to the dorm and read all about the *Wonders of the Universe* for a while before the bell rang.

He looked up at the great red brick clock-tower of the boarding-house. Frognal had told him Mr Knight was like the clock-tower and when he had asked why, Frognal had told him the clock had four faces but he still didn't understand. It was later than he had thought but it was only a short distance from the gate to the front door. He went in and hurried along to the dining room. No one else was around but there were still three buns left on the big tray surrounded by a confusion of used cups and saucers and small pools of spilt tea. Oliver took one of the buns and ate it, and then another, hesitating a moment before the third bun joined the gloves in his right-hand jacket pocket and he hurried out.

Upstairs, just outside the dorm, Oliver was surprised to hear voices. Nobody was meant to be up here at this time. He opened the door. Plummer and Bain and Meade were around Oliver's bed and the cupboard curtain was pulled back and the cupboard was empty and everything out of Oliver's cupboard was heaped on the bed in a tangled mess – books, clothes, everything.

'Hey, what do you think you're doing?' Oliver shouted as he rushed over and started to hunt through the pile of things.

'Don't make such a racket. We just thought we'd give you a little tidying up to do,' said Bain.

As Oliver found the photographs, Plummer added, 'Don't worry, we wouldn't steal your Mummy and Daddy.'

'Or your precious cook,' said Bain.

And then he heard Meade's voice saying, 'But look what I've got!' and he turned round and there was Meade holding the flag.

'Give me that!' Oliver tried to snatch it, but Bain and Plummer pushed him back on to the things on the bed and held him there.

'You know, it's not very patriotic keeping this thing. You are supposed to be English after all, even if you are a bit of a weirdo.' Meade reached into his trouser pocket and brought out the cigarette lighter.

'No, don't you dare!' Oliver shouted, but Bain and Plummer sniggered at his efforts to get away from them.

'It'll be so easy for you to get a nice Union Jack,' Meade said, his thumb flicking the little wheel on the lighter.

The bright colours brightened for a moment into flame and then the ashes drifted gently to the floor.

'My, my, the little twerp's crying!'

Graduation

EDWIDGE DANTICAT

The applause grew to a thunderous cry. Lights were almost blinding as I stepped into the crowded auditorium. I moved closer to the neat little row of seats on the stage.

'*Mamam*,' I whispered to my mother's soul and spirit that I carried in my chest, 'I am so very proud of you and *Papa*.'

The clip-clap-clap rose to its loudest possible, encompassing volume, reminding me of the strong Haitian rain as it beat rhythmically against the metal roof of my house and those of other houses nearby. I used to fall asleep bopping my head to the vibration of the rain as it forced itself on my roof. I never felt that serene doing anything else.

I took my seat next to two other well-dressed teenagers. Their satin caps and gowns glistened like well-polished silver coins officially decorated with the large head of the President for Life or the President Forever. I was happy to know that mine looked exactly the same.

'Now, ladies and gentlemen,' our principal said, turning quickly to face me, 'It is with great pleasure on this day that I present to you the most successful members of this year's graduating class. First, this year's valedictorian whose inspiring address you will soon have the pleasure of hearing – Miss Laperle Des Antilles.'

My heart beat so loudly that I could hear it and, if I wished, dance to it. I wished I were dancing, dancing elsewhere on top of a red and blue float of celebration, swaying my hands and smiling carelessly at a group of people who felt as much a glow of exhilaration as I. Instead, I was in a hot and jammed auditorium, filled with my bitterness. It was a bitterness like that nursed by the green and unwanted sugar cane, like that which overwhelmed the heart of an unripe and unobserved mango accidentally picked by a dry mountain rock.

The lights became unbearably blinding. As I tried to lift my feet to carry me to the podium so that I could recite my overly rehearsed valedictory address, I could not move.

'Mamam,' I pleaded. 'Give me strength.'

I felt more glued down than ever, as though a huge basket made by baked, starving, little brown hands had fallen on top of me and swallowed me.

'Papa, please help me,' I begged.

As soon as the words left my mouth, I saw blood in front of me. It was as red as that which came out of the necks of roosters when Papa sliced them. Pictures flashed about me in all types of vivid colours. Soon images floated in the air before me.

*

A young woman who worked with a small newspaper and wrote symbolic short stories about freedom and justice was naked in a dim, stenchfilled, tiny room where roaches, mice, and rats walked freely in and out. She hung by her wrists, and blood flowed from her neck.

Her hair – dark, coarse, and beautiful – was shaved and covered pieces of rotten bread and cheese on the foul floor. Every few minutes, she was stabbed by a cigarette and pierced with laughter.

'Say something now!'

'Criticize your leader now!'

'Tell me how badly we rule!'

Her tongue fell out, and she pleaded for mercy and water – mercy, but first, water. Every supplication was appeased by an excruciating, slow slash with a razored whip. Blood flowed until pieces of bread on the floor were soaked red. 'Your child is here! Here . . . watching! We'll have you all. We'll eat your whole generation. One . . . one . . . one by one.'

In my chest I prayed, *God, please let Mamam die.* She did not recognise me or else she would have read the request on my face. *Mamam, Mamam, please die.*

The basket was lifted momentarily, but I saw nothing except her face as it hung cowardly dripping of blood. She blew the blood away from her lips with hopeless, silent breaths.

Mamam, Mamam, please die.

I saw nothing until my face felt wet, as wet and cold as the poor

Haitian farmers' feet that never had anything but dry air between them and the brown soil. Water covered my face. I felt as though I was breathing my last breaths of air. I had no reason to go on, no reason to walk those last few feet to the beach. *Mamam* died last week.

We fled. *Papa* fell overboard from the little homemade boat we took from Haiti. We lost him to the vastness of the ocean.

A man on the boat yelled, 'No way will we give all the lives on this boat for just one life that's already lost anyhow!'

He did not even know my father.

'One death for one trip is a great success,' another said. 'Let us thank the gods.'

They thanked the gods joyfully.

My face was still wet when they put me in a filthy cell with two metal beds and six neighbours. We would go to Justice in a month.

*

No one nudged me or told me to get up. Perhaps they could no longer see me buried with my pain, paralysed on their stage, at my own high-school graduation. Tears forced their way out of my eyes. My heart beat louder than ever before in my entire life. I wanted my parents there with me.

*

I went before Justice smelling of avocado-coloured food they served the night before. I was so thin that my black skin fell in envelopes over my bones. After a month in the cells, men – who also came to Justice – had breasts bigger than mine.

Someone dressed in a navy-blue suit, carrying a black suitcase, said in a professional voice, 'These Haitians can't go back.'

'Why can't or don't you want to go back?' the judge asked me. 'Don't you love your native country? How can anyone claim any kind of attachment to the human race if he or she has no pride in the land that bore his or her ancestors?'

'I love no country – better or worse – more than I love my own country. It is a poor and oppressed country, but it is my country. I am here in your country because people in my own country will pluck the hairs out of my skin and stab me with fire simply because my family has criticized the corruption, thefts, and murders.'

No one could put my words in the judge's language. I knew he neither heard nor understood them. He did not want to hear or understand me.

People were around us – yellow, red, and almost beige. They acted as though they were not burdened with a burning wish to retell events that involved legal executions and human sacrifices. Yet they walked away with little square, green plastic cards.

I fell on my knees, devastated and destroyed. I pleaded in my Creole, 'Please let me stay. Please preserve me, harbour me, shield me, guard me, secure me, surround me, enclose me, house me.' I sighed to Justice. 'Justice. Please show me a little decency, I beg you. Come to my rescue. Save my life. They are bound to murder me. As soon as I set foot back on my soil, they will butcher me.

'They will slice me in fringed, little pieces, and their dogs will savage me. They will decapitate me and stare into my silent eyes where finally they will find weakness and shame. They will make me suck my own blood through the straws of my guts. Everyone who has ever spoken up will drink from me.

'No one will say anything. No one will know. The few who know will live only if they live in silence. I beg of you, give me that paper. Let me stay. Save me.'

I received no paper. I went as I came – to prison.

Sweet voices floated outside the basket trapping me. 'What so proudly . . . twilight . . . bright stars through some night.' Then some banners were waved over a land of the free and a home of the brave. Was I not brave enough?

A pastor came into the hell and prayed for me. I figured it was either the day before I would die or before I would be deported. I cried and vomited all the time, but no one came to help me. Finally the man with his Bible came. Was he the first of final rites? He asked me to confess all to God.

'Here, God, I confess all,' I said. 'I hate this earth and everyone on it. I even hate this man of religion you've sent to me, because I know that if you find him a throne to rule he will become evil. I hate everything and everyone and even you because you're evil for allowing people to become evil.'

I confessed that I wanted to go wherever *Mamam* and *Papa* were.

Whether above or below me, they could not possibly see as much evil as I would be forced to see.

Someone spoke. I barely heard the familiar voice, but I recognised the words. They urged self-love, pride, contentment, satisfaction. My valedictory address was full of the exact same words.

*

The pastor took me to his home; he had plenty of room. He took in three men and two women besides myself. My knees did not crack, and I did not vomit. Soon I could walk again.

I went to school and liked it, especially learning English. The sentences sounded like songs full of notes created with sounds of small rocks falling on large rocks in glass-clear streams.

I liked the school and really enjoyed the chicken lunches. Other children said, 'It stinks.' Sometimes I starved and did not eat the lunch so that they would not guess that in my country it could be a New Year's feast.

The children beat me and cursed me; they cursed my dress, my speech, my body, my hair, my Haitianness. I got special beatings for being Haitian. Sometimes, like *Mamam*, I bled. Like *Papa*, my dignity and claim to humanity drowned in salty waters.

*

Applause screamed with everything but bitterness. Happiness, pride, and love were all that drifted outside my tomb. Graduation, graduation – someone whispered how meaningful a step it was.

I was proud. I spoke good English; children beat me no more. I wore good clothes, uncoarsed my hair, and worked, too. I had more money than I needed. How Americanised I must have become.

A laugh echoed around me. Americanised? I? The AIDS carrier, the zombie, the voodoo beast, the caged, the homeless, the pitied, the despised, the feared, the ridiculed? And Americanised, too? That was only the dream.

'This day', the principal announced, 'is a milestone in all of your lives. As you sit here, you should be thinking about how hard you've worked to get where you are now. In small and, of course, limited ways, you should have relived parts of your yet-short lives which were for you the hardest of all.

'Cherish this moment in the perspective of how great and almost astronomical it is in the scheme of your lives. You have just begun. The sweeter parts of life remain ahead of you.

'Achieve it as you have achieved today, this great and wonderful day. A day which will prove more enlightening and marvellous if you all – graduates – go out with all intentions of changing the worst thing you have experienced in your lives so that all others yet to come will live to experience the difference you have made. Remember, those who know where they are going and remember where they come from can neither be lost nor stopped.'

Applause rose and rose until I visualised it lifting the roof a bit higher. The bodies rose as well. In a great wave of unison, a sweet, little song tingled in my ears.

I proudly carried myself out along with the other members of my class.

Antojos

JULIA ALVAREZ

The old aunts lounge in the white wicker armchairs, flipping open their fans, snapping them shut. Except that more of them are dressed in the greys and blacks of widowhood, the aunts seem little changed since five years ago when Yolanda was last on the Island.

Sitting among the aunts in the less comfortable dining chairs, the cousins are flashes of colour in turquoise jumpsuits and tight jersey dresses.

The cake is on its own table, the little cousins clustered around it, arguing over who will get what slice. When their squabbles reach a certain mother-annoying level, they are called away by their nurse-maids, who sit on stools at the far end of the patio, a phalanx of starched white uniforms.

Before anyone has turned to greet her in the entryway, Yolanda sees herself as they will, shabby in a black cotton skirt and jersey top, sandals on her feet, her wild black hair held back with a hairband. Like a missionary, her cousins will say, like one of those Peace Corps girls who have let themselves go so as to do dubious good in the world.

*

A maid peeks out of the pantry into the hall. She is a skinny brown woman in the black uniform of the kitchen help. Her head is covered with tiny braids coiled into rounds and pinned down with bobby pins. 'Doña Carmen,' she calls to Yolanda's hostess aunt, 'there are no matches. Justo went to Doña Lucinda's to get some.'

'*Por Dios*, Iluminada,' Tía Carmen scolds, 'you've had all day.'

The maid stares down at the interlaced hands she holds before her, a gesture that Yolanda remembers seeing illustrated in a book for Renaissance actors. These clasped hands were on a page of classic gestures. *The gesture of pleading*, the caption had read. Held against the breast, next to the heart, the same interlaced hands were those of *a lover who pleadeth for mercy from his beloved.*

*

The gathering spots Yolanda. Her cousin Lucinda leads a song of greeting with an off-key chorus of little cousins. 'Here she comes, Miss America!' Yolanda clasps her brow and groans melodramatically as expected. The chorus labours through the first phrase and then rushes forward with hugs, kisses, and – from a couple of the boys – fake karate kicks.

'You look terrible,' Lucinda says. 'Too thin, and the hair needs a cut. Nothing personal.' She is the cousin who has never minced her words. In her designer pantsuit and frosted, blown-out hair, Lucinda looks like a Dominican magazine model, a look that has always made Yolanda think of call girls.

'Light the candles, light the candles!' the little cousins say, taking up a chant.

Tía Carmen lifts her open hands to heaven, a gesture she no doubt picked up from one of her priest friends. 'The girl forgot the matches.'

'The help! Every day worse,' Tía Flor confides to Yolanda, flashing her famous smile. The cousins refer to their Tía Flor as 'the politician'. She is capable of that smile no matter the circumstances. Once, the story goes, during who-knows-which revolution, a radical young uncle and his wife showed up at Tía Flor's in the middle of the night wanting asylum. Tía Flor greeted them at the door with the smile and 'How delightful of you to stop by!'

'Let me tell you about the latest at *my* house,' Tía Flor goes on. 'The chauffeur was driving me to my novena yesterday. Suddenly the car jerks forward and dies, right there on the street. I'm alarmed, you know, the way things are, a big car stalled in the middle of the university *barrio*. I say, *César, what can it be?* He scratches his head. *I don't know, Doña Flor.* A nice man stops to help, checks it all – and says, *Why, señora, you're out of gas.* Out of gas! Can you imagine?' Tía Flor shakes her head at Yolanda. 'A chauffeur who can't keep a car in gasoline! Welcome home to your little Island!' Grinning, she flips open her fan. Beautiful wild birds unfold their silver wings.

At a proprietary yank from one of the little cousins, Yolanda lets herself be led to the cake table, festive with a lacy white tablecloth and starched party napkins. She dumb-shows surprise at the cake in the shape of the Island. 'Mami thought of it,' Lucinda's little girl explains, beaming.

'We're going to light candles all over,' another little cousin adds. Her face has a ghostly resemblance to one of Yolanda's generation. This one has to be Carmencita's daughter.

'Not all over,' an older brother says, correcting her. 'The candles are just for the big cities.'

'All over!' Carmencita's reincarnation insists. 'Right, Mami, all over?' She addresses a woman whose aging face is less familiar to Yolanda than the child's facsimile.

'Carmencita!' Yolanda cries out. 'I wasn't recognising you before.'

'Older, not wiser.' Carmencita's quip in English is the product of her two or three years away in boarding school in the States. Only the boys stay for college. Carmencita continues in Spanish: 'We thought we'd welcome you back with an Island cake!'

'Five candles,' Lucinda counts. 'One for each year you've been away!'

'Five major cities,' the little know-it-all cousin calls out.

'No!' his sister contradicts. Their mother bends down to negotiate.

*

Yolanda and her cousins and aunts sit down to await the matches. The late sun sifts through the bougainvillea trained to climb the walls of the patio, to thread across the trellis roof, to pour down magenta and purple blossoms. Tía Carmen's patio is the gathering place for the compound. She is the widow of the head of the clan and so hers is the largest house. Through well-tended gardens beyond her patio, narrow stone paths diverge. After cake and *cafecitos*, the cousins will disperse down these paths to their several compound houses. There they will supervise their cooks in preparing supper for the husbands, who will troop home after Happy Hour. Once a male cousin bragged that this pre-dinner hour should be called Whore Hour. He was not reluctant to explain to Yolanda that this is the hour during which a Dominican male of a certain class stops in on his mistress on his way home to his wife.

'Five years,' Tía Carmen says, sighing. 'We're going to have to really spoil her this time' – Tía cocks her head to imply collaboration with the other aunts and cousins – 'so she doesn't stay away so long again.'

'It's not good,' Tía Flor says. 'You four girls get lost up there.' Smiling, she indicates the sky with her chin.

'So how are *you four girls?*' Lucinda asks, a wink in her eyes. Back in their adolescent days during summer visits, the four girls used to shock their Island cousins with stories of their escapades in the States.

In halting Spanish, Yolanda reports on her sisters. When she reverts to English, she is scolded, '*¡En español!*' The more she practices, the sooner she'll be back into her native tongue, the aunts insist. Yes, and when she returns to the States, she'll find herself suddenly going blank over some word in English or, like her mother, mixing up some common phrase. This time, however, Yolanda is not so sure she'll be going back. But that is a secret.

'Tell us now exactly what you want to do while you're here,' says Gabriela, the beautiful young wife of Mundín, the prince of the family. With the pale skin and dramatic dark eyes of a romantic heroine, Gabriela's face reminds Yolanda of the lover's clutch of hands over the breast. But, Gabriela herself is refreshingly straightforward. 'If you don't have plans, believe me, you'll end up with a lot of invitations you can't turn down.'

'Any little *antojo*, you must tell us!' Tía Carmen agrees.

'What's an *antojo?*' Yolanda asks.

See! Her aunts are right. After so many years away, she is losing her Spanish.

'Actually it's not an easy word to explain.' Tía Carmen exchanges a quizzical look with the other aunts. How to put it? 'An *antojo* is like a craving for something you have to eat.'

Gabriela blows out her cheeks. 'Calories.'

An *antojo*, one of the older aunts continues, is a very old Spanish word 'from before your United States was even thought of,' she adds tartly. 'In fact, in the countryside, you'll still find some *campesinos* using the word in the old sense. Altagracia!' she calls to one of the maids sitting at the other end of the patio. A tiny, old woman, her hair pulled back tightly in a white bun, approaches the group of women. She is asked to tell Yolanda what an *antojo* is. She puts her brown hands away in her uniform pockets.

'*U'té que sabe*,' Altagracia says in a small voice. You're the one to know.

'Come now, Altagracia,' her mistress scolds.

The maid obeys. 'In my *campo* we say a person has an *antojo* when they are taken over by *un santo* who wants something.' Altagracia backs away, and when not recalled, turns and heads back to her stool.

'I'll tell you what my *santo* wants after five years,' Yolanda says. 'I can't wait to eat some guavas. Maybe I can pick some when I go north in a few days.'

'By yourself?' Tía Carmen shakes her head at the mere thought.

'This is not the States,' Tía Flor says, with a knowing smile. 'A woman just doesn't travel alone in this country. Especially these days.'

'She'll be fine.' Gabriela speaks with calm authority. 'Mundín will be gone if you want to borrow one of our cars.'

'Gabi!' Lucinda rolls her eyes. 'Have you lost your mind? A Volvo in the interior with the way things are!'

Gabriela holds up her hands. 'All right! All right! There's also the Datsun.'

'I don't want to put anyone out,' Yolanda says. She has sat back quietly, hoping she has learned, at last, to let the mighty wave of tradition roll on through her life and break on some other female shore. She plans to bob up again after the many *don'ts* to do what she wants. From the corner of her eye she sees Iluminada enter with a box of matches on a small silver tray. 'I'll take a bus.'

'A bus!' The whole group bursts out laughing. The little cousins, come forward to join the laughter, eager to be a part of the adult merriment. 'Yolanda, *mi amor*, you *have* been gone long,' Lucinda teases. 'Can't you see it!?' She laughs. 'Yoyo climbing into an old *camioneta* with all the *campesinos* and their fighting cocks and their goats and their pigs!'

Giggles and head-shakings.

'I can take care of myself,' Yolanda reassures them. 'But what's this other trouble you keep mentioning?'

'Don't listen to them.' Gabriela waves her hand as if scaring off an annoying fly. Her fingers are long and tapered; her wedding and engagement rings have been welded together into one thick band. 'It's easier this way,' she once explained, handing the ring over to Yolanda to try on.

'There *have* been some incidents lately,' Tía Carmen says in a quiet voice that does not brook contradiction. She, after all, is the reigning head of the family.

Almost as if to prove her point, a private guard, his weapons clicking, passes by on the side of the patio open to the back gardens. He wears an army-type khaki uniform, a gun swung over his shoulder. A tall wall has surrounded the compound for as far back as Yolanda can remember, a wall she believed as a child was there to keep the sea back in case during a hurricane it rose up to the hillside the family houses were built on.

'Things *are* looking ugly.' Tía Flor again smiles brightly. In the Renaissance book of acting, this grimace of a smile might be captioned, *The lady is caught in a smile she cannot escape.* 'There's talk, you know, of guerrillas in the mountains.'

Gabriela crinkles her nose. 'Mundín says that talk is only talk.'

Iluminada has now crept forward to the edge of the circle to offer the matches to her mistress. In the fading light of the patio, Yolanda cannot make out the expression on the dark face.

Tía Carmen rises to approach the cake. She begins lighting candles and laying the spent matches on the tray Iluminada holds out to her. One light for Santo Domingo, one for Santiago, one for Puerto Plata. The children plead to be allowed to light the remaining cities, but no, Tía Carmen tells them, they may blow out the candles and, of course, eat the cake. Lighting is grownup business. Once the candles are all ablaze, the cousins and aunts and children gather around and sing a rousing '*Bienvenida a ti*,' to the tune of 'Happy Birthday'.

Yolanda gazes at the cake. Below her blazes the route she has worked out on the map for herself, north of the city through the mountains to the coast. As the singing draws to a close, the cousins urge her to make a wish. She leans forward and shuts her eyes. There is so much she wants, it is hard to single out one wish. There have been too many stops on the road of the last twenty-nine years since her family left this island behind. She and her sisters have led such turbulent lives – so many husbands, homes, jobs, wrong turns among them. But look at her cousins, women with households and authority in their voices. Let this turn out to be my home, Yolanda wishes. She pictures the maids in their quiet, mysterious cluster at the end of the patio, Altagracia with her hands in her lap.

By the time she opens her eyes, ready, a half dozen little substitute puffs have blown out all the candles. There is a burst of clapping. Small arguments erupt over dividing the cake's cities: Lucinda's two boys both want Santiago since they went gliding there last weekend; Lucinda's girl and Carmencita's girl both insist on the capital because that's where they were born, but one agrees to cede the capital if she can have La Romana, where the family has a beach house. But, of course, La Romana has already been spoken for by Tía Flor's little goddaughter, who suffers from asthma and shouldn't be contradicted. Lucinda, whose voice is hoarse with disciplining the rowdy crew, hands Yolanda the knife. 'It's your cake, Yoyo. You decide.'

*

The road up through the foothills is just wide enough for two small cars, and so at each curve, as she has been instructed, Yolanda slows and taps her horn. Just past one bad curve, a small shrine has been erected, La Virgen surrounded by three concrete crosses recently whitewashed.

She pulls the Datsun over and enjoys her first solitary moment since her arrival. Every compound outing has been hosted by one gracious aunt or another, presenting the landscape as if it were a floor show mounted for her niece's appreciation.

All around her are the foothills, a dark enormous green, the sky more a brightness than a colour. A breeze blows through the palms below, rustling their branches, so they whisper like voices. Here and there a braid of smoke rises up from a hillside – a *campesino* and his family living out their solitary life. This is what she has been missing all these years without really knowing that she has been missing it. Standing here in the quiet, she believes she has never felt at home in the States, never.

When she first hears it, she thinks it is her own motor she has forgotten to turn off, but the sound grows into a pained roar, as if the engine were falling apart. Yolanda makes out an undertow of men's voices. Quickly, she gets into the car, locks the door, and pulls back onto the road, hugging her right side.

A bus comes lurching around the curve, obscuring her view. Belching exhaust, the driver saluting or warning with a series of blasts on his horn, it is an old army bus, the official name brushed over with paint that doesn't quite match. The passengers see her only at the last moment, and all up and down her side of the bus, men poke out of the windows, hooting and yelling, holding out bottles and beckoning to her. She speeds up and leaves them behind, the quiet, well-oiled Datsun climbing easily up the snaky highway.

The radio is all static – like the sound of the crunching metal of a car; the faint, blurry voice on the airwaves her own, trapped inside a wreck, calling for help. In English or Spanish? she wonders. That poet she met at Lucinda's party the night before argued that no matter how much of it one lost, in the midst of some profound emotion, one would revert to one's mother tongue. He put Yolanda through a series of situations. What language, he asked, looking pointedly into her eyes, did she love in?

*

The hills begin to plane out into a high plateau, and the road widens. Left and right, roadside stands begin appearing. Yolanda keeps an eye out for guavas. Piled high on wooden stands are fruits Yolanda hasn't seen in years: pinkish-yellow mangoes, and tamarind pods oozing their rich sap, and small cashew fruits strung on a rope to keep them from bruising each other. Strips of meat, buzzing with flies, hang from the windows of butcher stalls. It is hard to believe the poverty the radio commentators keep talking about. There seems to be plenty here to eat – except for guavas.

The fruit stands behind her now, Yolanda approaches a compound very like her family's in the capital. A high concrete wall continues for about a quarter of a mile. A guard rises to his post beyond an iron grillwork gate. He seems – glimpsed through the flowering bars – a man locked in a strangely gorgeous prison. Beyond him up the shady driveway is a three-storey country house, a wide verandah all the way around it. Parked at the door is a chocolate-brown Mercedes. Perhaps the owners have come up to their country home to avoid the troubles in the capital. They are probably relatives. The dozen rich families have intermarried so many times that family trees are tangles of roots. In fact, her aunts have given her a list of names of uncles and aunts and cousins she might call on along her way. By each name is a capsule description of what Yolanda might remember of that relative: *the one with the kidney bean swimming pool, the fat one, the one who was an ambassador.* Before she even left the compound, Yolanda put the list away in the glove compartment. She is going to be just fine on her own.

*

A small village spreads out before her – ALTAMIRA, say the rippling letters on the corrugated tin roof of the first house. A little cluster of houses on either side of the road, Altamira is just the place to stretch her legs before what she has heard is a steep and slightly (her aunts warned 'very') dangerous descent to the coast. Yolanda pulls up at a cantina, its thatched roof held up by several posts, its floor poured cement, and in its very centre, a lone picnic table over which a swarm of flies hover.

Tacked to one of the central posts is a yellowing poster for Palmolive soap. A creamy, blonde woman luxuriates under a refreshing shower, her head thrown back in seeming ecstasy, her mouth opened in a wordless cry.

'¡Buenas!' Yolanda calls out.

An old woman emerges from a shack behind the cantina, buttoning up a torn housedress. She is followed closely by a little boy, who keeps ducking behind her whenever Yolanda smiles at him. Asking his name drives him further into the folds of the old woman's skirt.

'You must excuse him, doña,' the woman apologises. 'He's not used to being among people.' People with money who drive through Altamira to the beach resorts on the north coast, she means. 'Your name,' the old woman repeats, as if Yolanda hasn't asked him in Spanish. The little boy mumbles at the ground. 'Speak up!' the old woman scolds, but her voice betrays pride when she speaks up for him. 'This little know-nothing is José Duarte, Sánchez y Mella.'

Yolanda laughs. A lot of names for such a little boy – the surnames of the country's three liberators!

'Can I serve the doña in any way?' the old woman asks.

'¿Un refresco? ¿Una Coca Cola?' By the pride in her voice, Yolanda understands the old woman wants to treat her to the best on her menu.

'I'll tell you what I would like.' Yolanda gives the tree line beyond the old woman's shack a glance. 'Are there any guavas around?'

The old woman's face scrunches up. '¿Guayabas?' she murmurs, and thinks to herself a second. 'Why, they grow all around, doña. But I can't say as I've seen any lately.'

'With your permission –' José Duarte has joined a group of little boys who have come out of nowhere and are milling around the car, boasting how many automobiles they have ridden in. At Yolanda's mention of guavas, he springs forward, pointing across the road towards the summit of the western hills. 'I know where there's a whole grove of ripe ones.' Behind him, his little companions nod.

'Go on, then!' His grandmother stamps her foot as if she were scatting an animal. 'Get the doña some.'

A few boys dash across the road and disappear up a steep path on the hillside, but before José can follow, Yolanda calls him back. She wants to go along too. The little boy looks towards his grandmother, unsure of what to think. The old woman shakes her head. The doña will get hot, her nice clothes will get all dirty. José will bring the doña as many guavas as she is wanting.

'But they taste so much better when you've picked them yourself.' Yolanda hears the edge in her voice. The old woman has turned into the long arm of her family.

The few boys who have stayed behind with José have again congregated around the car. Each one claims to be guarding it for the doña. It occurs to Yolanda that there is a way to make this a treat all the way around. 'What do you say we take the car?' The little boys cheer.

Now that is not a bad idea, the old woman agrees. If the doña insists on going, she can take that dirt road up ahead and then cross over onto the road that is paved all the way to the coffee barns. The old woman points south in the direction of the big house. Many workers take that shortcut to work.

They pile into the car, half a dozen little boys in the back, and José as co-pilot in the passenger seat beside Yolanda. They turn onto a bumpy road off the highway, which grows bumpier and bumpier as it climbs up into wilder, more desolate country. Branches scrape the sides and pebbles pelt the underside of the car. Yolanda wants to turn back, but there is no room. Finally, with a great snapping of twigs and thrashing of branches across the windshield, as if the countryside is loath to release them, the car bursts forth on to smooth pavement and the light of day. On either side of the road are groves of guava trees. The boys who have gone ahead on foot are already pulling down branches and shaking loose a rain of guavas.

Yolanda eats several right on the spot, relishing the slightly bumpy feel of the skin in her hand, devouring the crunchy, sweet white meat. The boys watch her.

The group scatters to harvest the guavas. Yolanda and José, partners, wander far from the path that cuts through the grove. Soon they are bent almost double to avoid getting entangled in the thick canopy of branches overhead. Each addition to Yolanda's beach basket causes a spill from the stash already piled high above the brim.

*

The way back seems much longer than the way there. Yolanda begins to worry that they are lost, and then, the way worry sprouts worry, it strikes her that they haven't heard or seen the other boys in quite a while. The latticework of branches reveals glimmers of a fading sky. The image of the guard in his elaborate flowering prison flashes through her head. The rustling leaves of the guava trees echo the warnings of her old aunts: you will get lost, you will get kidnapped, you will get raped, you will get killed.

Just ahead, the thicket of guava branches clears, and there is the footpath, and beyond, the gratifying sight of the car still on the side of the road. It is a pleasure to stand upright again. José rests his burden on the ground and straightens his back to full measure. Yolanda looks up at the sky. The sun is low on the western horizon.

'The others must have gone to gather kindling,' José observes.

Yolanda glances at her watch – it is past six o' clock. At this rate, she will never make the north coast by nightfall. She hurries José back to the car, where they find a heap of guavas the other boys left behind on the shoulder of the road. Enough guavas to appease even the greediest Island *santo* for life!

They pack the trunk quickly, and climb in, but the car has not gone a foot before it lurches forward with a horrible hobble. Yolanda closes her eyes and lays her head down on the wheel, then glances over at José. His eyes are searching the inside of the car for a clue as to what could have happened. This child won't know how to change a flat tyre either.

Soon the sun will set and night will fall swiftly, no lingering dusk as in the States. She explains to José that they have a flat tyre and must go back down the road to the big house. Whoever tends to the brown Mercedes will surely know how to change a tyre.

'With your permission,' José offers. The doña can just wait in the car, and he will be back in no time with someone from the Miranda place.

Miranda, Miranda. . . . Yolanda leans over and gets her aunt's list out of the glove compartment, and sure enough, there they are. *Tía Marina y tío Alejandro Miranda – Altos de Altamira*. A note elaborates that Tío Alejandro was the one *who used to own English saddle horses and taught you four girls to ride*. 'All right,' she says to the boy. 'I'll tell you what.' She points to her watch. 'If you're back by the time this hand is over here, I'll give you' – she holds up one finger – 'a dollar'. The boy's mouth falls open. In no time, he has shot out of his side of the car and is headed at a run toward the Miranda place. Yolanda climbs out as well and walks down a pace, until the boy has disappeared in one of the turnings of the road.

*

From the footpath that cuts through the grove on the opposite side of the road, she hears the sound of branches being thrust aside, twigs snapping underfoot. Two men, one short and dark, and the other slender and light-skinned, emerge. They wear ragged work clothes stained with patches of sweat; their faces are drawn. Machetes hang from their belts.

The men's faces snap awake at the sight of her. Then they look beyond her at the car. The darker man speaks first. 'Yours?'

'Is there some problem?' he speaks up again. The taller one is looking her up and down with interest. They are now both in front of her on the road, blocking any escape. Both – she has sized them up as well – are strong and quite capable of catching her if she makes a run for it. Not that she can move, for her legs seem suddenly to have been hammered into the ground beneath her. She considers explaining that she is just out for a drive before dinner at the big house, so that these men will think someone knows where she is, someone will come looking for her if they try to carry her off. But her tongue feels as if it has been stuffed in her mouth like a rag to keep her quiet.

The two men exchange a look – it seems to Yolanda – of collusion. Then the shorter, darker one speaks up again. 'Señorita, are you all right?' He peers at her. He is a short man, no taller than Yolanda, but he gives the impression of being quite large, for he is broad and solid, like something not yet completely carved out of a piece of wood. His companion is slim and tall and of a rich honey-brown colour that matches his honey-brown eyes. Anywhere else, Yolanda would find him extremely attractive, but here on a lonely road, with the sky growing darker by seconds, his good looks seem dangerous, a lure to catch her off her guard.

'Can we help you?' the shorter man repeats.

The handsome one smiles knowingly. Two long, deep dimples appear like gashes on either side of his mouth. '*Americana*,' he says to the darker man, pointing to the car. '*No comprende.*'

The darker man narrows his eyes and studies Yolanda a moment. '¿*Americana?*' he asks her, as if not quite sure what to make of her.

She has been too frightened to carry out any strategy, but now a road is opening before her. She clasps her hands on her chest – she can feel her pounding heart – and nods. Then, as if the admission itself loosens her tongue, she begins to speak, English, a few words, of apology at first, then a great flood of explanation: how it happens that she is on a back road by herself, her craving for guavas, having never learned to change a flat. The two men stare at her, uncomprehending, rendered docile by her gibberish. Only when she mentions the name Miranda do their eyes light up with respect. She is saved!

Yolanda makes the motions of pumping. The darker man looks at his companion, who shrugs, baffled as well. Yolanda waves for them to follow her. And as if after dragging up roots, she has finally managed to yank them free of the soil they have clung to, she finds she can move her own feet toward the car.

The small group stands staring at the sagging tyre a moment, the two men kicking at it as if punishing it for having failed the señorita. They squat by the passenger's side, conversing in low tones. Yolanda leads the men to the rear of the car, where they lift the spare out of its sunken nest – then set to work fitting the interlocking pieces of the jack, unpacking the tools from the deeper hollows of the trunk. They lay their machetes down on the side of the road, out of the way. Above them, the sky is purple with twilight. The sun breaks on the hilltops, spilling its crimson yolk.

Once the flat has been replaced with the spare, the two men lift the deflated tyre into the trunk and put away the tools. They hand Yolanda her keys.

'I'd like to give you something,' she begins, but the English words are hollow on her tongue. She rummages in her purse and draws out a sheaf of bills, rolls them up and offers them to the men.

The shorter man holds up his hand. Yolanda can see where he has scraped his hand on the pavement and blood has dried dark streaks on his palm. '*No, no, señorita. Nuestro placer.*'

Yolanda turns to the taller one. 'Please,' she says, urging the bills on him. But he too looks down at the ground – Illuminada's gesture, José's gesture. Quickly, she stuffs the bills in his pocket.

The two men pick up their machetes and raise them to their shoulders like soldiers their guns. The tall man motions towards the big house. '*Directo*, Mirandas.' He enunciates the words carefully. Yolanda looks in the direction of his hand. In the faint light of what is left of day, she can barely make out the road ahead. It is as if the guava grove has grown into the road and woven its matt of branches tightly in all directions.

She reaches for each man's hand to shake. The shorter man holds his back at first, as if not wanting to dirty her hand, but finally, after wiping it on the side of his pants, he gives it to Yolanda. The skin feels rough and dry like the bark of trees.

Yolanda climbs into the car while the two men wait a moment on the shoulder to see if the tyre will hold. She eases out on to the pavement and makes her way slowly down the road. When she looks for them in her rearview mirror, they have disappeared into the darkness of the guava grove.

*

Ahead, her lights catch the figure of a small boy. Yolanda leans over and opens the door for him. The overhead light comes on; the boy's face is working back tears. He is cradling an arm. 'The *guardia* hit me. He said I was telling stories. No *dominicana* with a car would be out at this hour getting *guayabas*.'

'Don't you worry, José.' Yolanda pats the boy. She can feel the bony shoulder through the thin fabric of his shirt. 'You can still have your dollar. You did your part.'

But his shame seems to obscure any pleasure he might feel in her offer. Yolanda tries to distract him by asking what he will buy with his money, what he most craves, thinking that on a subsequent visit, she might bring him his own little *antojo*. But José Duarte, Sánchez y Mella says nothing, except a mumbled *gracias* when she lets him off at the cantina with several more than his promised dollar.

In the glow of the headlights, Yolanda makes out the figure of the old woman in the black square of her doorway, waving goodbye. And above the picnic table on a near post, the Palmolive woman's skin gleams a rich white; her head is still thrown back, her mouth still opened as if she is calling someone over a great distance.

PART IV

Questions and Essay Suggestions

A Note to Teachers

Discussion questions are designed to elicit discussion of the following basic elements of short fiction: structure, plot, setting (scene), characterisation, description, point of view, theme and symbolic language. Students are expected to understand the underlying structure of a short story, e.g. climax (turning-point) and dénouement, and terms such as foreshadowing, preparation, motivation, conflict, foils, epiphany, dialogue, frame and flashback, omniscient narrator, first-person narration and limited omniscient narrator.

Essay questions, while deemed worthy of more consideration than classroom time would ordinarily allow, could profitably be used in classroom discussion as well, if preferred.

Questions and Essay Suggestions

Lily, They Said

1 When is the story set? What clues does the author furnish?
2 The story is a fantasy of sorts, but is the main plot (Lily's naiveté and her pregnancy) believable in its historical context?
3 Senior's writing style is unusual. What are its characteristics? Does it help or hinder the reading of the story?
4 Unlike most stories, there is no dialogue. Where would you put dialogue?
5 What is the central idea or theme of the story, i.e. how does the plight of a man differ from that of a woman in the Caribbean?
6 What does the story reveal about colonialism? About class differences and colour?

Essays
1 Describe Lily's future.
2 Could this story take place in the 1990s?

Ah Liberated Man

1 How would you characterise the relationship of the married couple? How do the two couples act as foils (point up the differences between them)?
2 How old do you think Manjack and Soursop are? Do they seem to be similar in any way?
3 Do the women sound like they're from Trinidad? Is the language authentic? Is the dialogue between the characters believable?
4 Children play a very insignificant role in the story. Why?
5 What does the title mean?
6 What do you think of how Manjack was manipulated? Should his new wife have been more honest and straightforward?
7 This is a first person narration. How would it have been different if Manjack had told the story?

Essay
Do you think this is simply a humorous fantasy or are values really changing in the Caribbean? How are they changing?

Miss Joyce and Bobcat

1 What do you know of Miss Joyce's personality? Of Bobcat's? How are they different?
2 The author is very careful to describe the setting. Why is it significant here?
3 Do you find it plausible that they would like each other? Were you prepared for the ending?
4 This story is told from what is called a limited omniscient narrator point of view (third-person but generally more from one person's perspective, in this case, Miss Joyce's). How would it be different if told from Bobcat's point of view?
5 What is the theme? Don't give a plot summary but consider the message the author wants us to grasp.

Essays
1 Do you think their relationship has a future? Imagine their lives five years hence.
2 The story shows such insight into Miss Joyce's character that you may be surprised to know the story was written by a man. Do you think men can write about women with real understanding?

Baby

1 Why is the story entitled 'Baby'?
2 Miss Sweetie is far from the stereotype of a selfless midwife. What are her main qualities?
3 Do you have sympathy for Miss Sweetie or do you find her feelings reprehensible?
4 What is your response to Easton, the father of Veena's sixth child?
5 Were you surprised by the ending? Did the author prepare you adequately?
6 Note the opening description in its use of colour, of light and dark imagery.
7 This is an extremely tight short story. Do you feel you need to know more about any characters?
8 Although we learn about the setting, the author tells us nothing of the time frame. When do you suppose the story is set?

Essay

Easton is upset that his new baby is a girl. Did his response seem familiar to you? Why does he feel this way? Is this an old-fashioned response or not?

The Occasional Sadhu

1   How is the sadhu described?
2   Do the religious details help or hinder the story?
3   How does the fact that this is a first-person narrator and the narrator is a child affect your reading of the story? Do you have a reliable narrator here? How might the sadhu himself tell this story?
4   Does the young boy (the narrator) change as a result of meeting the sadhu?
5   What is the turning-point (climax) of the story?

Essay

Have you ever known anyone who has 'made the journey' the narrator speaks of, to 'loss of fortune, family disputes, diminution of power'? Write about such a person who went through a spiritual or physical transformation. Describe him or her before and after.

Pan for Pockot

1   We never meet Mister Harris, only hear his cough, and hear of his opinions through Lady Emelda. Why? What does he represent symbolically?
2   Note the physical description of the people and the physical surroundings, the birds particularly, and the preacher.
3   Irony plays a big role here. Pockot keeps playing 'Jerusalem, the Golden' and Pockot's mother is called Lady Emelda.
4   How does the story reveal Trinidad's many cultures and prejudices?
5   How realistic is the description of Trinidadian street life?
6   Do you have sympathy for Pockot? Mister Harris? Lady Emelda?
7   What is the turning-point (climax) of the story?

Essay

Is the ending negative or positive for Pockot?

The Dark Side of Being Nine

1   Olivese constantly criticises Branwell's mother. Was this a smart thing to do, considering she feels his mother is better than his father? What is her motivation? What does it reveal of her character?

2 What do we know of Branwell's mother and father? What are their main personality traits?
3 Olivese has tried for three years to change Branwell. Has she succeeded?
4 Is it likely that Olivese could keep her plans to move to England secret?
5 Are you prepared for the ending? Does Branwell's suicide seem likely, considering his personality and the circumstances?
6 What finally convinces Branwell to commit suicide and imitate the way his father killed a dog?
7 Where is the conflict here?

Essay
In 'Pan for Pockot', Pockot is booted out of his house and here Branwell commits suicide because his mother is sending him away and Olivese is leaving for England. Compare and contrast the two situations and the outcomes for the two young boys.

Exile

1 This story is written in the present tense whereas most stories are not. How does that affect your reading of it?
2 How is climate used to augment the story's theme? Note the many references to cold, wind and snow, and how setting is used as contrast.
3 How English has Desmond become? What hints do we have? Why is his Englishness significant for the story's outcome?
4 Were you adequately prepared for the ending?
5 How is London contrasted with Clemencia? How significant is it that London is a real place and Clemencia is fictitious?
6 What is the turning-point (climax) of this story? When does the action change?

Essay
Obviously Desmond is bitter, but is his characterisation of island politics as 'back-biting nastiness' accurate?

Flying the Flag

1 Why is it 'important not to cry'? What finally makes Ollie cry?
2 The flag is the flag of the newly-independent island, and the British boys burn it. What is the symbolism here?
3 How is Ollie different from the other boys? What are his major characteristics?

4 There are a lot of conflicts going on in the story: conflicts between the day boys and the boarders, the old boarders and Ollie, between British and island values. How are they all related?

5 This is a 'frame story' in that it begins with Ollie walking back to the school then goes into a flashback and returns to the present with Ollie late getting back for tea. How does this work for you? How else might the author have structured the story?

6 Is the dialogue believable?

7 Why is it ironic that Ollie has bought a book entitled *Wonders of the Universe*?

Essay
In what way does this story deal with the issue of colonialism?

Suggested Reading
Voyage in the Dark by Jean Rhys.

Graduation

1 The author uses a great many metaphors in her work. Note their use and particularly those that make reference to fruits or situations that are particular to the Caribbean.

2 This is a frame story, like 'Flying the Flag', in that it begins and ends in the high-school auditorium, but past and present often intertwine. Reality is mixed with the narrator's memory. Did you find the distinctions clear? How else might the narrator have written the story? Does this structure work for you?

3 The narrator, Miss Laperle des Antilles, mentions the way she was treated upon first arriving in America. Is she exaggerating? Have you heard of or experienced such prejudices yourself? How is it different, if at all, when Caribbean peoples move to England?

4 The memories of Haitian torture are frightening and horrific. From your readings, are they realistic?

Essay
Why is the title 'Graduation' a particularly good choice? From what, besides high school, is the narrator graduating?

Antojos

1 How does the story portray class differences in the Dominican Republic?

2 How do the different generations respond to the troubles on the island?

3 What is the significance of Yolanda pretending to be American?
4 Explain these symbols: the Palmolive woman, the guavas.
5 Note the description of the guava grove. Why is that important to the story?
6 Where is the conflict in the story?

Essays

1 Like many Caribbean people, the narrator, nicknamed, significantly 'Yoyo' has left her homeland. Returning is never an easy transition. Will Yolanda stay in the Dominican Republic or return to the States?

2 How does this story examine, along with other themes, the feelings of powerlessness among women?

PART V

Notes on the Authors

Notes on the Authors

Julia Alvarez was born in the Dominican Republic. After receiving her undergraduate and graduate degrees in literature and creative writing, she spent twelve years teaching poetry in American schools and in Nicaragua. *How the Garcia Girls Lost Their Accents* was published in 1991 by Algonquin Books of Chapel Hill and was named a *New York Times Book Review* and American Library Association Notable Book of the Year. She now lives in Vermont and teaches at Middlebury College.

Edwidge Danticat was born in Port-au-Prince, Haiti, but grew up in Brooklyn, New York. She has a BA from Barnard College, and is in the process of completing a Master's Degree in Fine Arts at Brown University. She is a poet, playwright, screenwriter and translator as well as a fiction writer. She won second prize in the *Seventeen Magazine* Fiction Prize, and her work has been published in a number of literary magazines. Her novella on Haiti will soon be published in an anthology called *Womyn* [sic] *in Exile*.

John Gilmore was educated in Barbados and at Cambridge University. He has taught in the history department at the University of the West Indies (Cave Hill), was Cultural Officer for Literary Arts at the National Cultural Foundation in Barbados and is now managing editor of *Caribbean Week*. He has published academic and popular articles as well as the biography, *The Toiler of the Seas: A Life of John Mitchinson, Bishop of Barbados* and co-authored *A–Z of Barbadian Heritage*. His poetry and short stories have appeared in *Bim*, *Kyk-Over-Al*, *The New Voices*, *Poetry Review*, and *Graham House Review*.

Vjange Hazle was born in Jamaica and attended Mico Teachers College there. Her stories have appeared in *The Sunday Gleaner*, *Focus 1983* and *The Caribbean Writer*. She now lives in Connecticut.

Anthony Lockhart attended school in Antigua and Dominica and at the University of the West Indies in Jamaica and Barbados. He is currently Chief Education Officer in Dominica. Previous publications include *Two Heads* with Arundell Thomas (1974) and *Man in the Hills* (1984). He is at work on a novel.

Rabindranath Maharaj, born in Trinidad, completed his MA in English at the University of the West Indies, St Augustine, and has been working as an English literature and language teacher in Trinidad for the past twelve years. His short stories have appeared in *The Caribbean Writer* as well as the *Trinidad and Tobago Review*. A book of his stories is soon to be published by Peepal Tree Press, England.

E. A. Markham, from Montserrat, is senior lecturer in Creative Writing at Sheffield Hallam University. He has directed the Caribbean Theater Workshop, been a media coordinator in Papua New Guinea and held writing posts in universities, colleges and schools. His books of verse are *Human Rites, Living in Disguise, Lambchops in PNG,* and *Towards the End of a Century*. He edited *Hinterland*, the *Bloodaxe Book of Caribbean Verse*, and *Something Unusual*, a book of stories, appeared in 1986. As a literary editor, he has been involved in the editing of *Ambit* and has edited *Artrage* and *Writing Ulster*. His forthcoming books are *Letter from Ulster* (poetry) and *Neighbours from St Caesare* (stories) and his play *The Narrative Verandah* has been produced in London.

Lionel Seepaul was born in Waterloo, Trinidad and graduated with a BA in English from Laurentian University in Ontario, Canada. He has written for the BBC, has published in *Short Story International, London Magazine, Minerva Anthology* and was included in *Best Short Stories 1988*, as well as *The Caribbean Writer*. Presently, he lives in Vancouver.

Olive Senior was born and educated in Jamaica. She is the author of six published books, including two short-story collections, *Summer Lightning* which won the Commonwealth Writers Prize in 1987, and *Arrival of the Snake-Woman*, and a poetry collection, *Talking of Trees*. She has also published the *A–Z of Jamaican Heritage* and most recently, *Working Miracles, Lives of Women in the English-Speaking Caribbean*.

Jonathan Small was born in Barbados and educated at the University of the West Indies (Jamaica), Rutgers University, and the University of Pittsburgh, and is currently a professional librarian in Barbados. He has published two collections of poetry and has just finished a novel.

Marvin E. Williams was born and raised on St Croix in the United States Virgin Islands and attended Cornell University for his BA and Master's Degree in Fine Arts. Formerly a lecturer at the Africana Studies and Research Center at Cornell University, he is currently a visiting professor at the University of the Virgin Islands. Previous publications include *The Caribbean Writer, Caribbean Quarterly, Collage Two* and *Okike*.